Rewind

An adventure in time travel, a search for the truth!

Copyright 2001

Revision 2 2017

Keith Finley

Acknowledgment

Born and raised in a small town in South Carolina, book publishing never entered my mind until 2001. Rewind was a result of a conversation between me, and my coworkers that we had during our lunch break, at a local automotive parts manufacturing plant located in Anderson, South Carolina. It started as a conversation about the space shuttle sighting that was to occur during our lunch break. We would plan our lunch break around the sightings time that occurred each night. During the conversation, I brought up some story that I found on the internet, about the John F Kennedy assassination, and a light went off like it was sent from above. After we went back inside to begin work, I sat down at the computer and typed out the synopsis. The idea was born and five months later my book "Rewind" an adventure in time travel, a search for the truth was completed. I hope you enjoy my first book and may the truth about that dreaded day come to light. My theory of the assassination is included in this book, it also includes some research that I did during my nights of searching on the Internet. My thanks to my friends that worked with me in Anderson, and to their rave reviews that kept this book alive.

Rewind

An adventure in time travel, a search for the truth!

Pilot John Snow, copilot Dale Dazzler, payload specialist Lori Miller, and team physician Dr. Fredrick Jarvis are being suited up for a routine space flight. NASA is only hours away from the launch of its new space shuttle called "prospector," when what should be a routine maiden flight, turns into an adventure in time travel, a search for the truth. The shuttle with only seconds from reaching outer space develops problems, and the crews last minute decisions takes the high-tech craft back to November 21, 1963. With their high-tech camcorders, radios, and camera, the crew is faced with several decisions, which might alter history. Should they stop the assassination of President John F Kennedy, or sit back and watch it happen? With all the facts, and a few modern marvels, the team sets out on a journey where there is no turning back. What they discover is the hidden mystery of that fatal day in Dealey Plaza that no one has been able to figure out before now. It's a journey that you will never forget!

Chapter One

It is a warm sunny day in Florida as the new space shuttle "prospector" readies for its maiden voyage. The prospector is one of the space program's most complex space vehicle, and its four-crew members are preparing for a six-day flight. The crew will dock with the new space station called Freedom. Pilot John Snow, copilot Dale Dazzler, payload specialist Lori Miller, and team physician Dr. Fredrick Jarvis are being suited up for the maiden voyage. John is a captain in the United States Air Force. He has over ten years of flight experience; and he will lead this mission which will deliver the medical research module to the new space station. Dale Dazzler was a pilot during the Gulf War and was stationed on the Aircraft carrier John F Kennedy. Dale was mission specialist on the mission that deployed the solar array to the space station in November 2000. Doctor Fredrick Jarvis will conduct new experiments that deal with cell reproduction that occurs after a patient has had radiation treatment for cancer. Fredrick worked at the advanced research center for cancer located in Maryland. If these tests are successful, they could help the fight against cancer, which kills millions of Americans each year. Lori Miller is in charge of deploying the new module which she has been training on for several months. Lori a southern belle from South Carolina, has always dreamed of flying in space, and finally after five long years of training will get to use her honed skills on the shuttle prospector maiden voyage. After several days of bad weather, the skies have cleared and the lift off time has been set for 2pm. With only minutes left to go before launch, the team has left the flight briefing room and is headed to the launch site, which is labeled 40a. The launch team specialists are busy getting the four-crew members buckled in for their fiery launch, which will take this modern marvel to its marriage with space. The team is extremely happy because all of their hard work and dedication is about to pay off in one of the most amazing liftoffs that Florida has ever seen. This shuttle is the first to take off like an airplane; the earlier missions have had to rely on the external tanks, which have become common place with past missions. The shuttle also has the new advanced cabin deployment system, which, if used, will save the crew if the shuttle has a malfunction, the crew's cabin will eject from the space shuttle and glide safely back to the earth. This shuttle cost less to operate because of the new advanced engine designed built in Southern California. If this modern marvel is successful, the cost of flying it will be as cheap, as the operation of the new Concord Airliner which no longer flies today. The team is ready and the countdown clock is ticking with less than four minutes to go. The shuttle is responding well and all the system appear to be ready for flight. John strapped snuggly into the pilot chair watches the dials, and monitors all the flight systems as the fiery beast comes to life as it readies for its maiden flight. John looks over at Dale and says, "just think we are about to find out what the phrase space cowboys mean!" Dale replies, "just think we get to fly this wonderful craft first!"

The flight Director calls for the retraction of the emergency escape system, which signals that launch, is only seconds away.

John comes over the capcom and replies "the

emergency escape system has clear the shuttle; all

systems are go for takeoff!"

Mission control replies, "roger prospector, clock

shows twenty-five seconds to go."

The launch director interrupts the capcom and
replies,

"emergency landing sites are clear, and on standby,

prospector you are go for launch!"

John replies, "all systems are go, all is clear, and

we are standing by!"

Finally, the command center begins to count
"fifteen, fourteen, thirteen, twelve, eleven, ten,

Mission control replies, go for main engine start

nine, eight, seven, six, five, the engines begin to

fire and the shuttle comes to life as a dragon spraying fire. The craft begins to tremble, four, three, two and one, the ground shakes, and the shuttle screams down the runway, and into the beautiful Florida sky. A stream of smoke follows the modern marvel as the space center fades slowly out of sight. John comes over the capcom and replies, "engines are at sixty-five percent, all systems are go!"

The launch Director replies, "prospector is 26 miles down range, speed velocity is two thousand miles per hour, emergency landing site in Spain is on standby, all is well and we are standing by for, go at throttle up command from mission control!"

Mission control replies, "roger.... prospector you are go for throttle up,"

John replies, "roger Houston we are go for throttle up." John grabs the throttle, and with a jolting thump, the throttle is at one hundred percent. The speed of the craft accelerates and the crew is driven back into their seats as the mighty prospector, roars clean out of sight. As the craft reaches the upper atmosphere it begins to peek into the pitch darkness of night that sits on the edge of space. The launch director comes over the capcom and says, "prospector's engines are at one hundred percent, prospector is fifty-six miles down range, speed velocity is five thousand miles per hour, emergency landing site in White Sands is on standby!"

After twenty minutes of flight the shuttle is committed to its voyage, it has also reached the point, considered to be the most dangerous. With only seconds to go until it passes this point, fire begins to race pass the nose of the new craft which signals that the craft is leavings Earth's atmosphere. All seems well except that Dale has noticed a warning light which has appeared to signal trouble for the craft and crew. Dale looks over at John and replies, "John we have a problem, engines three and four are overheating!"

John looks over and he sees the light glowing brighter and brighter.

John gets on the capcom to Houston and says,

"Houston we have engines three and four are over

heating please advise!"

 Mission control has noticed that the main engines

have begun to overheat, and the sensors are

determining to shut the main engines down.

Houston's Capcom replies, "roger prospector

please stand by!"

 John who is beginning to sweat looks over at Dale

and says, "this don't look good, we are going to

have to shut those engines down very soon!"

John comes over the Capcom and says, "Houston engines three and four are overheating, we need permission to shut them down, please advise!"

John reaches for the flight manual that explains what task he needs to do in order to abort the mission and land the craft at the nearest emergency landing zone. Dale who is awaiting word from Houston, begins to reach for the shutdown switch, as the Capcom suddenly lights up with a worried voice replying, "okay prospector you are go to shut those two engines down, you are clear to abort the mission and your destination will be White Sands New Mexico!"

Suddenly Dale hits the switch and the craft's engines shuts down and the craft glides through the darkness of space. The nearest landing zone is located 5000 miles at White Sands Air Force base in New Mexico. John whose mind and hands are working double time, looks over at Dale and says, "Dale we need to begin to switch the main computer over to the emergency landing software, while you do that I will begin to change our course and begin to reenter Earth's atmosphere!"

Dale replies, "I'm two steps ahead of you, emergency software is loaded and is ready when you are!"

John who continues to watch all flight systems, and is changing the craft's course, notices that the radio is only filled with static. Dale looks over at John, and John looks over at Dale, both in total disbelief. John reaches for the Capcom and says, "Houston are you there, this is prospector!"

Silence fills the Capcom, when after a few seconds has gone by,

Dale replies, "Houston this is Prospector, how do you read!" Silence continues to fill the Capcom when John says in a solemn voice, "I guess it's up to us now, the radio is dead and we are on our own!"

If John doesn't take control shortly, the craft might burn up in the upper atmosphere, and the crew will become ashes, which will be sprinkled all over the Pacific Ocean. So, he reaches for the emergency flight manual, that gives the coordinates to the landing zone in New Mexico. The manual also confirms the designation and the angle of reentry so that he will be able to land the craft successfully. If he uses the wrong entry angle, the spacecraft could bounce off and be thrown into outer space, or burn up into the earth's atmosphere and become a memorial to space. John and Dale will perform fifteen minutes of delicate flying in order to bring the crew and craft to a safe landing. Once the craft has reached twenty thousand feet, the level of danger decreases as the craft breaks the speed of sound. Dale rechecks the coordinates and the crew proceeds to enter the Earth's Atmosphere, their speed is well above normal, but Dale is more concerned with the angle of entry than of the speed of the craft. Because of the trembling and shaking of the craft, Dale is thrown into the dashboard and his arm hits several switches, which cause the craft to spin out of control.

John reaches for the control lever to try to bring the spacecraft in line with the navigation chart and compass heading, which are given in the flight plan. A bright fiery ball of fire races past the nose of the craft, which becomes so bright that it blinds John and Dale for a few moments causing them to lose sight of the instrument panel. The craft continues to shake, as the blue sky comes into view, causing the crew to give a sigh of relief, because they have almost made it through the fifteen minutes of danger. Within minutes the crew tries to spot the chase planes which follows the craft to the dry lakebeds located at White Sands. Suddenly a warning light appears which signals a drop-in cabin pressure. Because of the shaking and trembling from the crafts reentry, the cabin has cracked causing the warning light to appear. John who is excessively sweating, replies, "we aren't going to make it! We are going to have to hit the emergency cabin deployment and leave this

baby!"

Dale replies, "okay you guys prepare for cabin
deployment!"

  The crew tucks in their feet into the foot restrains
and each crew member attaches their oxygen to the
self-contained oxygen supply which is located
inside the cabin.

John comes over the radio and says, "okay you
guys get ready, as he starts counting five, four,
three, two, one, Dale go for cabin deployment!"

Dale hits the switch and there is a loud explosion

and the cabin detaches from the spacecraft, and the

crews cabin heads for the desert floor below. The

three billion-dollar shuttle streams through the sky

as if it was a duck wounded in flight. It begins to

tumble and then a horrendous explosion lights up

the sky as the last piece of the modern marvel fall to desert floor below.

About that time Dale replies, "that was and expensive fireworks display."

The cabin parachutes deploy, and slowly the cabin begins to sail like a glider. John reaches for the flight manual and looks under the emergency landing procedures to see if he can find the coordinates needed to find the dry lakebeds. After flipping through several pages, he notices that the coordinates are nowhere to be found. The space program hasn't landed a shuttle anywhere else since they built the four-mile landing strip in Florida back in 1987. After several minutes of looking out the window, John sees a very small strip that looks like it might be their final destination. He reaches for the flight controllers and sails the craft leading it towards the small strip that he just spotted out the window moments ago. Because of his military training that John has received, he will use his honed skills to land the craft safely. He points the craft towards the small strip which increases in size as the craft gets closer to their final destination. The wheel touches the ground, and the cabin shakes with a jolting thump. Johns applies the brakes, which slows the cabin to an unprecedented and sudden stop. The crew notices that the recovery team hasn't arrived to help them escape. So, the crew opens the hatch and slowly descends to the dry lakebed below.

The crew still in disbelief because of the lack of the recovery team presence, causes them to wonder if the recovery team knows exactly where they are, so they continue to try the radio but all they receive is static. The cabin is full of provisions, which was loaded for the six-day trip in space. John gets out and takes a walk around the detached cabin when he notices a large billow of smoke coming from the horizon. John replies, "hey you guys look, there is our 3 billion-dollar fire burning over there that must be the crash site of the shuttle."

The crew begins to exit their space suits and begin to reach for their sky-blue flight suits, which are a lot lighter and more comfortable than the bulky space suits they wear during liftoff. Once the crew has dressed, they continue to waits until after an hour has passed before the crew decides to leave the detached cabin. Each crew member packs their duffel bag, which contains their personal items along with a few provisions, and they begin walking towards the nearest road. John the ship's captain reaches into the storage compartment, and gets several headsets that are radios, which the crew can use to communicate to each other while they are on the ground. He also gets a camcorder plus extra batteries and tape that was going to be used during the space walk, and during their flight. John replies, "Heck you never know what we might come across out here in the desert."

John shuts the cabin's door, and the crew set out walking until they reach about 500 yards from the landing site. Since the recovery team hasn't arrived, flight rules state that if they must leave the detached cabin, it must be destroyed to prevent someone from stealing NASA's latest technology. Then John reaches in his flight suit and pulls out a remote control. The remote will destroy the cabin

and there will be nothing left after the explosion.
John looks over at the crew and says, "okay you
guys get yourselves down, and I'm going to blow
the cabin!"

John hits the button on the remote control and the
cabin explodes and after the smoke clears, there is
nothing left but a pile of rubble. After about a half
of a mile walking down the nearest road, they see
an old man driving a truck coming down the road
towards them. The crew begins to wave at him as if
to signal him to stop. The old man slows to a stop
and asks the crew where they are headed. John
introduces himself and explains their problem and
asks the man if he has a cell phone they can use.

The man replies, "I don't know anything about a cell phone, but I can give you a ride into town to use the telephone."

The crew erupts in laughter and John replies, "sounds good to me!" The crew climbs in the back of the truck and down the road they go. The old man introduces himself and tells John about his garage that he has own for over twenty years. His name is Bill Davis, a native of Texas who moved out to the desert when he was a young man. He runs a garage and most of his business comes from tourist that visit the Air Force base that is located a short distance from his home. The old truck is a sixties model Ford pickup which appears to be in mint condition. John ask Bill about his truck, and why it looks so new, Bill replies, "I just purchased it from a new car dealer located in the small town, located about thirty miles up the road."

Bill goes on to brag about the radio, power steering, power brakes and the nice ride that the truck has. John asked him how much did you pay for it, Bill replies, "two thousand and some change."

John was amazed at the price because his father had one restored some years back, and it cost over ten thousand to restore the old truck. Bill asked John "do you want to listen to the new radio that has come with the truck."

John replied, "sure there might be some news on the radio that might let them know what happen to their trip into outer space."

Bill reaches over and turns the volume up, and they are listening to a local radio station out of Odessa. The announcer was talking about a president who was visiting Texas, there in the next few days, he stated that it was the first time in years that the president had visited the state. John looked over at Bill and says, "what president are they talking about?"

Bill smiled and said, "well heck everyone knows who the president is, his name is John F Kennedy!" John screams " stop the truck Bill...stop it now!"

John jumps out the truck and yells "Dale, Lori, Fredrick, did you hear that announcement!"

 The crew replies "what was that all about?"

 John replies "something bad has happened, we are in 1963, and John F Kennedy is visiting Texas in the next few days."

Bill who looks totally confused says, "what in the world is going on here John?"

John who looks delirious says "Bill have a seat there is something I must talk to you about."

John proceeds to tell Bill about the spacecraft, and the troubles they had while in flight. Bill whom appears nervous and troubled about the story replies "You guys have got to be kidding me"

John shaking his head replies "nope I'm serious and we are going to need your help."

Bill replies "heck I'm just an old mechanic who works on cars for a living, what can I do to help you guys!"

Well we need your help to get to Dallas Texas before the president gets there because he will be killed by an assassin's bullet there in the next few days. Bill gasps "you guys have got to be kidding me"

John replies nope, president Kennedy was killed in the motorcade on November the twenty-second, and we are going to try to stop it!

Fredrick replies "you guys will never believe what I have in my duffel bag."

So, he reaches into his duffel bag and pulls out a copy of the book titled "The *Truth about John F Kennedy Assassination:* my sister bought me this book for my birthday, and I took it with me on the trip!"

 Dale's eyes light up with excitement as he flips opens the book.

John speaking up says "if we go through this crazy idea we might alter history, and if we do that there is no telling what might happen!"

Bill reaches over and grabs the book and opens it to see if these guys are on the level. Bill's eyes open wide, and he starts looking at the pictures in the book, he turns and says "this is unbelievable, how in the world could we stand back and let something like this happen."

Lori nodding her head says "we can't, we are talking about the president of the United States here!"

Chapter Two

John who is completely puzzled by the whole situation replies, "how are we going to get to Dallas? And we don't have any money, how are we going to survive something like this?"

Bill nods and replies, "okay you guys let go to my house, where we will change cars, and I have some money saved up and I will get us to Dallas."

So, the crew loads up in the truck and down the road they go, headed towards Bill's house, where they will change cars and pick up some extra money for the trip to Dallas.

After twenty minutes or so the crew arrives at a small farmhouse located on the edge of the Air Force base. It's a picture out of the history books, a simple wooden home, nothing fancy except the old cars parked around the garage. There are fifties, sixties and even several old Pontiac's, parked near the house.

John replies, "I wished I had a camera so I can take pictures of this!"

Lori squeals "wait a minute I have a digital camera in my duffel bag let me see if I can find it!"

Bill replies "a digital camera? What the heck is a digital camera?" Lori replies, "It's a camera that takes colored pictures and saves them to a memory

34

disk, it's a computerize image, that makes the

picture look sharper and clearer, than the old film

type."

 Bill replies "Colored pictures! All we have is black

and white ones, gosh that sounds interesting."

Lori takes the camera and starts taking pictures

of everything, when Dale replies "Lori you better

save the batteries because I don't think we can

find some AAA batteries around here!" Lori

says, "yep you are right we better save them

because we might need it in Dallas."

About that time John says, "don't worry, I brought

a camcorder with extra memory cards, and extra

batteries!"

Lori replies, "you got to be kidding, let me see that camera, no one is going to believe these pictures." After a few minutes of filming Bill's farm, Bill invites the travelers to come in and have a late lunch. His wife Maggie has just prepared a nice meal, which consists of fried chicken, rice and gravy. As they sit at the table Maggie asks them where are they from and what are they doing at their house. John speaks up and says" we are test pilots for the space program, we are testing out a new space craft which was launched on its maiden voyage today. The engines overheated and we had to abort the mission, so we landed here at White Sands emergency landing strip."

Maggie replies, "heck you are nowhere near White Sands, you are at Odessa Air Force base in Texas! I don't believe in that space stuff, I think it is a waste of money!"

John says, " well a lot of folks don't understand the purpose of the test but let us say that no one can compete with the Americans, we will land a man on the moon, and the USA will have a space plane and it will be called the shuttle!"

Dale speaks up and says " John, I think they have heard enough about the future, lets finish this fine meal, we have a long trip ahead of us."

The team finishes the nice meal and goes outside

and sits on the front porch and begin their

discussion on the upcoming trip to Dallas.

John looks at Bill and says, "Bill how long will it take to get to Dallas?"

Bill replies " my guess is about a six-hour drive

from here, but I can get you there in about 4 hours,

I know all the back roads, and short cuts!"

John speaks up and says "Bill are you sure you

want to do this? Because we don't want to tie you

up in our business and take you away from your

work that you have here."

Bill replies " I wouldn't miss this for the world" I

haven't seen any excitement around here since

1954, and I'm not about to miss this trip!"

So, the team starts preparing their gear for the trip, Dale turns and asks Bill " what car will we be taking to Dallas?"

Bill replies "well we will need plenty of room, so let's take my Ford van, it has plenty of room, and I just rebuilt the engine last week."

So, the team loads up the van and Bill kisses his wife and says, "Honey I will be back in a few days"

Maggie his wife says, "you are not going anywhere without me, I'm going too!"

she jumps in the van, and the team is headed off to Dallas.

Chapter Three

After a few minutes of traveling John looks at Bill and says" have you told her what we are about to do?'

Bill replies, "nope I figured we had plenty of time to tell her as we head towards Dallas!"

Lori speaks up and says " let me tell her and I will get her up to speed on our mission!"

Lori tells the whole story to Maggie as the team speeds down the old country roads to Dallas. Lori squeals " Doc she has fainted!"

 Bill stops the van and has Doctor Fredrick jumps out and starts checking on Maggie to see if she is okay. Fredrick reaches into his medical bag and pulls out some smelling salts and tries to wake Maggie up, she jumps and yells " You guys have got to be kidding me, there is no way this is happening!"

Bill replies " honey it's the truth, and we are going to help these guys, it's the least we can do."

Fredrick replies "Maggie you will be all right, you just fainted from the excitement."

Bill continues the trip and away they go, headed towards Dallas. After a few miles of silence Maggie looks at Lori and says "I can't believe that this is happening to us."

Lori nods "well we don't believe it either!"

About that time Dale speaks up and says, " I know how we are going to stop the assassination from happening, we will block the motorcade, and cause it to take another route so that it doesn't go near the schoolbook depository building and the grassy knoll. Also, we will stake out the schoolbook depository, and the grassy knoll, and find out who were the actual killers were. This book I'm reading is unbelievable, it has all the details about the assassination and it even provides pictures and a map of Dallas."

About that time Doctor Fredrick speaks up and says," just think, I might be able to save the presidents life if he does get shot, since I know all the latest medical procedures!"

Bills looking in the rear-view mirror and says" I can't believe we are going through with this, this is the most exciting thing since we drop the bomb on Japan and ended the war!"

John replies " well it's not that big, but the only drawback is, we might be changing the history as all of us know it. We might be sticking our hands in something we shouldn't be, but as for my two cents worth I think that this is a great idea!"

Fredrick Responds, "I wonder if we can go a little further and try to contact the secret service and tell them about the assassination attempt."

Dale speaks up and says, "are you kidding, first off they wouldn't believe the story if a priest was to tell them, furthermore, how do we know that they aren't involved with the killing themselves!"

Lori nods in agreement and replies "I'm not sure anyone would believe our story, even if we have a book to prove it."

Bill who has been listening very attentively replies "if we don't pull over soon we will have to walk to Dallas, I need to gas up the van, and get something to drink at the next gas station we come to."

So finally, after a few miles the crew comes upon a gas station located several miles from Abilene Texas. Dale who has been carrying the camera since the crew left Bill's house squeals "look you guys it's a scene from Happy Days, it's an Esso

station, and look gas is only 22 cents a gallon!"

Bill who jumps out of his wits replies "gas has

always been between 25 and 20 cents, what's the

big deal about it being 22 cents?"

Dale replies "Bill we have to pay $1.85 a gallon for
unleaded, and $2.05 a gallon for premium
gasoline."

Bill gasps "a dollar eighty-five you got to be

kidding me, there is no way I would pay that for a

gallon of gasoline."

Dale replies "well if you were living in the year

2017 you would, and by the way there will be a gas

shortage in 1975, and everyone will be effected!"

Lori who is giggling in the background replies "you guys are killing me, remind me next time to bring a lot of cash with me, I could be a rich woman living in these times!"

Fredrick says, "I wished I had a copy of all the winners of the Kentucky Derby for the next ten years with me, now that would be the scheme for being a rich man!"

John screams "okay you guys knock that stuff off, we have a mission to do here, we are already knee deep in altering history, we don't need to be swimming in it!"

Chapter Four

The team is over whelmed by the little town store, cokes are a dime, and even a pack of Cigarettes is 15 cents. The store is filled with old pictures of world war two; even an old poster of *"uncle Sam wants you"* is pasted on the wall. As you enter the store, penny candy lines the counter; the cash register is the old push button type something out of the fifties. Dale who is completely awed by the current situation, asks the man running the store "how long have you owned this store?"

The old man squeaks "my dad started this store in the early twenties and it's been mine since 1952."

Dale replies "well I really like it, and it's a picture out of the history books!"

The old man puzzled by the Response replies "well I wouldn't take anything for it, I have met a lot of folks here, plus a president even stopped by here once, and that was Harry Truman."

Dale smiles brightly and says, "did you get an autograph?"

The old man replies "Yep, and that's it hanging on the wall!"

Dale runs over to see it, and it's a scene out of the old history book that he remembers during his time in grade school, a picture of Harry Truman visiting the memorial at Pearl Harbor. John interrupt and says, "come on you guys we have to get going." He reaches over and hand's the man five dollars for gas, and replies "have a good day sir and thanks for the memories!"

The old man nods and says "thank you and come again!" Bill wheels the van out of the store, and up the road they go, Dale replies "can you believe this trip, I have gotten the opportunity to visit the nineteen forties, nineteen fifties, and nineteen sixties, all in one day, this is unbelievable!" Lori interrupt's the conversation and says sarcastically, "yes and just think we are all from the future, and on a mission to alter history!"

So, the van speeds down the old tar and gravel road heading towards Dallas, only one day to go before the historical visit, and a time to prepare everyone for the events that are soon to follow.

Dale who is continuing to read the book sets the timeline of events.

He replies, "okay you guys here are the plans, first off we will need to cause a traffic accident at the intersection that will prevent the motorcade from going down Dealey Plaza, this will occur at 12:30pm. The shots were fired between the time of 12:35pm, and 12:40pm, also we will need someone to stake out the school book depository, and the grassy knoll. Also, I have heard from other sources that there may have been other shots from the man hole cover located in front of where Zapruder was filming the whole event. Now we want the doctor to be in a place that he could cover the possibility of a shooting if it happens. But if we do this thing right, no one will get shot and we might finally know the real truth about the assassination attempt."

Lori speaks up and says, "this is so weird for us to know that something like this is going to happen, and then sit back and watch this event unfold right before our eyes."

Then about that time Doctor Fredrick looks at Dale and asks, "are there any details about the type of wounds he received? And if so how many did he have?"

Dale replies, "well he took one shot near the back of his neck, and that shot might have exited through the throat, then there was the head shot and appeared to come from the grassy knoll, it was known as the fatal shot that took off part of his head!"

The doctor replies "well I know I can deal with the gunshot to the neck, but is there any details about the head shot that gives any more information about brain damage, or any other information to the extent of the wound to the head?"

Dale replies "no not really, just that the head shot was considered being, the decisive blow."

The doctor replies, "well let's just make sure that if he does get shot, it's not to the head, because there isn't much I can do."

Bill interrupts and asks, "why would anyone want to kill the president, and who was behind this terrible deed?"

Dale replies, "well after years of investigations the incident no one has found anything that places the blame on anyone, there were some reports that the CIA was behind it some even offered evidence that the mob had him killed!"

Bill replies, "well whoever is behind it, we will try to disrupt their plans, just think we might be able to prove who actually did kill him once we stake the whole crime scene out!"

John who has been quiet for some time looks at Dale and says, "Where do you think would be the best place to take pictures with the digital camera that we have?"

Dale replies "I think the opposite side of the street that the motorcade is on, and that way we can get a picture of the sixth-floor window, that Oswald was in during the shooting. Furthermore, we need a shot of the grassy knoll, and of the manhole cover located where the motorcade was before we altered the route. What we want to do is avoid Dealey Plaza, and re-route the motorcade from Elm Street, then have someone in the key areas of where the proposed assassination was to take place."

John interrupt and says, "I brought along a camcorder where would be the best place to film the whole event, since we are going to be high tech here we might as well do it right!"

Dale replies, "what about the overpass that the motorcade passes under after the shooting, there you would have access to the whole crime scene!"

John replies, "that's a great idea, and with its 24 times zoom that it has I can get a close-up of everything."

Lori speaks up and says, "that sounds great, but I want to cover the schoolbook depository, I want to see how Oswald gets in, and how he gets out."

Dale replies "I will take the grassy knoll, I want to see if anyone who looks suspicious is found in that area, if so I will let you know."

Fredrick replies "I guess I will be the cameraman, and I will try to position myself where I can catch all the action!" Maggie who is completely dumb founded replies, "what am I supposed to do? I have to cover something."

 Dale replies, "well we need someone to cause the traffic accident on Houston Street, so would you want to do that?"

Maggie replies, "sure count me in!"

Bill who is driving the truck says, "there is a motel, about two miles ahead, I guess we will stop here for the night."

John replies "how far from Dallas are we?"

Bill replies, "about forty miles!"

John replies, "let's get as close to Dallas as we can, that way we will be ahead of traffic in the morning!"

Bill continues to drive when after about an hour they arrive in Dallas. Dale breaks the silence and says, "looking at the map here in this book; it appears to show a motel about three blocks from Dealey Plaza. That is where we need to spend the night."

Bill replies "sounds good to me, it's been a long day for me."

So, the team arrives at the motel which is only minutes from Dealey Plaza, Bill takes the van and parks it behind the motel, and the crew settles in for a long-awaited rest. The team notices that there is a small restaurant located beside the motel, so the crew goes in and sits down and prepares to order supper. The crew orders the usual hot dogs, hamburgers and continues to talk about the day's events. Finally, John looks over at Lori and says, "well you guys I've had enough for today, I will catch you in the morning."

John and the rest of the team gets up, John picks up the tab and everyone heads towards the motel. Right before the team splits up Dale replies, "okay you guys we will all meet at the restaurant in the morning, how about eight o'clock"

Everyone nods in agreement, and the team splits off, and heads towards their rooms, and then off to bed.

Chapter Five

The team awakes and prepares to get itself ready for the midday visit that is only four hours away. At last report the president's plane would be arriving sometime around 12 o'clock noon in Dallas. The team is at the local restaurant eating breakfast as Dale picks up the morning paper. Dale replies "man look at these headlines, everybody is in a swirl about the visit, even the local paper is covered with it."

John who looks over a cup of coffee replies, "I just hate that there is going to be more to those headlines than what is currently in them."

About that time the waitress asks the team what they want for breakfast, when she is interrupted by the old black-white TV, and of course the TV is filled with the story too. The waitress replies, "boy are they driving this in the ground or what, it seems that the most important things are taken a back seat to this mess."

Dale looks over to her and replies, "yep you are right, but you never know when this story might take another turn and become something that is historic in content."

About that time Fredrick walks up and says, "are you guys ready for the big day, I haven't slept all night!"

John replies, "you too huh, seem there is a lot of that going around these days!"

John looks over to the waitress and says, "How far away is Dealey Plaza from here?"

The waitress replies, "about three blocks, you will have to turn at the red light onto Houston Street and the next left is Elm Street, then you will be there."

The waitress looks at Dale with this big grin and says, "but you better get over early, because everyone in Dallas will be there too!"

Dale replies, "I wouldn't miss this motorcade for the world, this is a once in a lifetime event."

The waitress squeals, "gosh what is so important about a president visiting here, I lived in

Washington DC for two years and I passed them on the freeway like they were standing still!"

The waitress walks away shaking her head when John replies, "I would love to see her face in the morning!"

About that time Lori walks up and joins the others at the table and she say, "I feel terrible it must have been the bed last night, I didn't sleep a wink."

John replies, "Lori I don't think anyone can sleep knowing what we all do, it was a long night for everyone!"

Fredrick speaks up and says, "you guys we need to put a cap on this and get ourselves out to Dealey plaza, we have a busy day ahead of us!"

The team finishes their breakfast and Bill pays the tab, and they head off towards Dealey Plaza with only two hours to go. About that time Lori speaks up and says, "hey you guys we need to change our clothes; we need to change into something else that doesn't look so obvious!"

So, the team spots a used clothes outlet about two blocks down from the restaurant. The team walks in and looks for some dark clothes that will help them fit in with the local crowd. After about 30 minutes has passed the team leaves the clothes outlet and they appear to look like the local citizens of Dallas. Lori who is surprised by the clothes she is wearing replies, "now I know why my mother complained about these clothes. They sure weren't built for comfort."

Dale replies "my goodness I look like my Uncle Jed he always wore coveralls."

So, the team heads down to Dealey Plaza to check out the crime scene before the crowd arrives. Within minutes a strange silence comes over the team as they walk into view of the deadly crime scene. John who looks over toward the grassy knoll replies, "man this is unreal, look at this place, it is the perfect setting for an ambush."

 Lori speaks up and says, "look you guys there is the schoolbook depository, and up on the sixth floor is the snipers nest!"

Dale whose eyes are staring at the grassy knoll replies, "I think over there behind the fence would provide the best cover for an assassin, look at the shadows over there, you can't see anything over there."

Bill and Maggie looked over and Maggie replies, "there is a deathly feeling about this place, it's almost like walking into a crime scene after it has already happened!"

Bill replies, "yep you are right Maggie, it's a funny feeling to be standing here, knowing that something bad is going to happen within the next hour."

John who reaches into his duffel bag replies, "yep and just think we are prepared this time around, the snipers will get caught this time if all goes as planned."

John looks over at Doctor Fredrick and says, "doc what do you think about this crime scene?"

Fredrick replies, "I can't believe I'm standing here, look over there what are those men doing!"

The team looks over and notices that a black car as pulled up over next to the grassy knoll, then three men in dark trench coats appear and they start walking towards the picket fence located near the grassy knoll. Lori replies, "do you think that they are with the Secret Service?"

Bill replies, "I bet so!"

When Dale replies, "well I don't know about you but I'm going over there and see what's up!"

About that time John speaks up and says, "wait a minute Dale, I have something for you."

John reaches in the duffel bag, and pulls out two headsets and hands one to Dale and John replies, "here put this on and let me know what you see when you get there."

Dale replies, "where did you get those headsets, I didn't know you had brought them with us?"

John replies, "I picked them up from the storage compartment on the shuttle, I figured we might need them once we were on the ground."

Dale puts on the headset and he does a sound check to make sure they are working properly. John puts on a set and talks into the microphone and says, "Dale how do you read?"

Dale replies, "loud and clear!"

Lori looks over at John and says, "how many sets did you bring?" John replies, "six, I thought I would bring all of them, since there might be a possibility of one or two of them malfunctioning." Lori speaks up and says, "well give me a set, I'm going over to the schoolbook depository and have a look around!" John reaches into the duffel bag and pulls out a headset and hands it over to Lori. Lori takes the headset and starts putting it on and

Dale voice comes over the headset and says, "okay you guys I'm over here fixing to cross Elm Street and I'm headed to the grassy knoll, how do you read?"

John replies, "loud and clear Dale your radio sounds great." Lori starts walking towards the schoolbook depository and John replies, "well we might as well start getting into place, and we only have 45 minutes to go before he arrives."

So, the rest of the team starts getting ready to go and get into their position for the motorcade when Maggie replies, "Hey you guys how am I supposed to cause a traffic accident?"

John replies, "take the car and position yourself at the intersection of Houston and Main Street, then right before the motorcade arrives take the car and block the street, pretend that it has stalled in the middle of the road."

Maggie replies, "okay sounds great, I'm an expert on choking down a straight drive, especially our old Ford van!"

Bill looks over to Maggie and says, "after it chokes down, raise the hood and pull the coil wire off the distributor and let it hang down, then after the motorcade passes I will come over and fix it."

John looks over at Maggie and says; "now it's up

to you to change the motorcade route and make sure that the limousine takes the alternate route!" Maggie looks over at John and says "right boss, consider it done."

John reaches over and hands Maggie a headset; he goes on to show her how it operates. John replies, "okay Maggie here is how this thing works, put this ear piece in your ear, and clip the mike to your shirt, the radio clips on your belt, but be sure to cover it with your shirt. The mike is voice activated so be careful what you say because we will all be able to hear it."

John reaches into the duffel bag and hands Fredrick a headset, and replies, "here doc, you're wired and ready to go!"

John looks over to Bill and says, " Bill I want you to walk up about a block or two above Houston Street, and you yell at Maggie on the radio when it's time for her to block the road!"

Bill replies, "you got it captain, I'm on my way!"

Chapter Six

With everyone headed to his or her place at the deadly crime scene John prepares himself for what is to come. He begins to talk to all the team members by the radio, making sure that everyone is aware of what they are going to do. John takes a deep breath and says, " okay ladies and gentlemen first off can everyone hear me?"

Dales replies, "yep loud and clear."

Lori replies, " yep got you here."

Fredrick replies, " John you sound great!"

Bill takes a deep breath and says, " sound good to me."

Maggie says, " over and out!"

John replies, "Okay, here is the plan, Bill will give us the green light, he is stationed about two blocks down, and he will let Maggie know when she needs to block the intersection. Then Maggie will block the intersection of Houston and Main, Bill will run up the road and help Maggie get the car started, once the motorcade has been rerouted. Bill, you will get the car started and you will park the car behind the schoolbook Depository. Lori, you will follow Lee Harvey Oswald from the schoolbook depository to where ever he goes once the motorcade has passed. If something was to go wrong and the Motorcade makes the deadly trip through Dealey Plaza, then Lori you follow him wherever he runs off to. Now if someone else is the sniper then follows him and Bill and Maggie will follow you as support. Lori if you need any help then Dale is located at the grassy knoll, behind the fence is a railroad yard; it should lead up behind the schoolbook depository where you can help Lori. I'm positioned on the overpass, which overlooks the whole Plaza. Doctor Fredrick is located opposite side of the street from the grassy knoll; he will use the digital camera and take pictures of the schoolbook Depository, and the motorcade. Doc the sniper was located on the extreme right corner, sixth floor. Try to get his picture, and watch all the activity from that direction. If the president gets shot you run towards the motorcade and tell the Secret Service that you are a doctor and you are there to help. We will pick you up at the hospital later. Also watch the grassy knoll, the head shot might have come from there, if you see anything-suspicious take a picture of it. Get all the pictures you can of anything that looks out of place. Remember we must keep ourselves undercover, don't let anyone think that we might be up to something, because if we do, we might get the blame here, and there is no telling what kind of trouble we will wind up in. I will film the whole crime scene. I will cover every piece of real estate I can. Everyone needs to stay calm, and don't do anything that puts you at risk! Dale will support me if I need it, and be sure to keep your eyes and ears open, there is also a possibility of the sound bouncing off the walls. So just because a shot appears to come from a certain direction, doesn't make it official, be sure to look for smoke or a muzzle flash. Now does everyone understand what your role is and what you are to do?"

Lori replies, " yep!"

Dale replies, " you got it!"

Fredrick says, " I'm ready."
Bill and Maggie replies at the same time and says, "we got it and good luck everyone!"

John looks at his watch and the team has about fifteen minutes to go. John replies, "Okay team everyone set your watch to 15 minutes

from...Now!"

 The team sinks their watch and John says, "Okay

Lori what do you have going on at the

Depository?"

 Lori replies, "okay I'm at the front door, there is a lady at the desk,

I will ask to see Lee."

 Lori walks up and asks the lady at the desk," I'm here to see

Lee Oswald, is he here?"

The old lady replies, " yes he is, he is in the

second-floor break room eating lunch!"

Lori replies "okay thanks have a nice day!"

Lori proceeds toward the stairs when she tells Bill,

" Okay I'm headed up to the second floor, this place is spooky."

John replies, " just be careful and watch your step!"

Dale comes over the radio and says, " well our three guys in trench coats are nowhere to be found, and they have just vanished."

John replies "they have to be there somewhere, try behind the fence."

Dale walks over to the fence, and he sees three men standing next to a black automobile, two is dressed in plain clothes, and one has own a policeman's uniform, it appears that they have taken off their trench coats and placed them in the back of the car.

Dale replies, " yep your right, they are there, and they have changed clothes, plus they have taken off their coats."

 John replies "okay sounds good follow them and see what they are up to."

Dale replies, " okay I'm on my way!"

So, he walks up close to them and he is within ten feet of them, one of the man says, " hold it right there, what are you doing back here?"

Dale replies, " oh just looking for a good spot to see the president!"

The man replies, " Well I'm a secret service agent, these guys here are with the Dallas Police department, we are roping off this area to keep you spectators away from this area!"

Dale replies " let me see your badge!"

The man replies, " I don't have to show you anything, now clear this area or we will haul you in!"

Dale replies "sure boss whatever you say!"

Dale turns and walks back towards the grassy knoll when he replies, " John did you hear that?"

John replies," yep I sure did, find a good place and watch those guys and see what they are up to!"

About that time Lori comes over the radio and says, " okay you guys I see him, he is over there eating lunch, he looks nervous, it appears that he is really keeping an eye on his watch."

Lori says, " I will talk to him, hold on and let's see how he acts!"

John replies, "Lori you be careful, he might be dangerous!"

Lori walks over to him and says, "hey are you Lee Oswald?"

Lee replies, "yep who wants to know?'

Lori replies "I do, and a friend of mine told me that you could get me a copy of a history book at a cheap price!"

Lee replies, " yep what edition do you need?"

Lori with the expression of surprise says, " well I'm a senior at a local college, and I need one for this semester, can you help!" Lee replies, well yes but we will need to go to the sixth floor to get it!" Lori replies sure no problem I will follow you!"

Lee gets up, and him and Lori heads for the stairs, and up to the sixth floor they go. John comes over the radio in a whispering voice and says, Lori be very careful, and watch your step!"

Lee takes Lori up to the sixth floor and she notices another man sitting by the window she walks over to him and says, " man this is an excellent view for the motorcade!"

The man replies, ' yep but I'm no fan of the president, I'm from Cuban descent, and he hates my people!"

Lori replies, " I don't believe that, I think he just doesn't like your leader that's all!"

The man replies, " well we will see what happens today; he will get a wakeup call today!"

Lori replies, " what do you mean a wakeup call?

The man looks at Lori with an evil grin and says,

" just wait you will see!"

About that time Lee says, " do you want this book?

Do you have five dollars?"

Lori replies, " well I don't today, I was only

interested in seeing if you could get it, but I will

pay you tomorrow."

Lee replies, " well I will hold it for you, but you

will need to pay me tomorrow if you want the

book, I can't hold it forever!" Lori replies, " okay

sounds great, by the way can I stay up here and

watch the president's motorcade with you?"

Lee replies, " sure there isn't anything exciting

going to happen anyway so grab a box and have a

seat!'

Lori pulls up a box and sits down next to Lee and

prepares to watch the motorcade. John who has

listened to the whole conversation whispers, " Lori

look out the window and see if you see anything

suspicious going on."

Lori gets up and leans out the window and she
gazes out the window and scans Dealey Plaza. As
Lori looks over towards John's location she sees
him and Lori replies, " Boy there is sure a lot of
folks here today, they are lined up everywhere,
even near the overpass."

The other man sitting near her replies, " yep and all

this just to see a lousy president. I'm sure glad he

isn't mine, I would rather shoot him that salute him!"

Lee laughing in the background says, " he wouldn't be worth that much trouble, you would have the Secret Service all over you for that!"

The man replies, "well it sure would make my country proud of me they can't stand him."

About that time another man walks through the door and says, "hey Lee! I need to see you a moment."

Lee replies, "sure what's up Jim, you are a tad early you said that you would be here at 1:00pm."

Jim replies, "well I figured that since we were going to have the president's visit, the trip would take me longer, but I found a shortcut and got here earlier."

Lee replies, "did you bring the money?"

Jim replies, "yep here you go, and you did say forty dollars, right?"

Lee replies, "yep and here is the gun."

Lee opens the long package and several empty shell casings fall to the floor and there in the packaging was the Italian bolt action rifle that was found by the police back in 1963. Lori whose eyes are as big as a saucer exclaims, "Lee don't you think that this might be a bit risky since the president is only moments away!"

Lee replies, "well I need the money, that is the only reason I'm selling the gun!"

Lori exclaims, "well what about the casings being on the floor, if something happens you will be the first suspect that they will come after then what are you going to say?"

Lee replies "I have worked for the CIA they won't bother me they know I'm clean."

Jim looks over at Lee and says, "Lee can I leave the gun here until after the president motorcade has left?"

Lee replies, "sure I will lie it over here behind these boxes, you can pick it up later!"

John who has been listening to the whole story whispers to Lori and says, "Lori get out of there, there is no reason for you to stay, we know the story!"

Dale who has been listening to the radio communications replies, "Lori check out that building across the street from the schoolbook depository, maybe that is where the shots came from!"

Chapter Seven

So as the team listened to the radio communication between Lori and Lee, Fredrick replies, " hey you guys I think there is some commotion coming from the Dal-Tex building located across the street beside the schoolbook depository! I see someone located on the second floor, the second window from the right, it appears to be the only window raised on that floor!"

Lori who hears this from the ear piece replies "Hey you guys I need to get going it's has been nice talking to you."

Lee looks over at Lori and says, "will you be back tomorrow? I thought you wanted to watch the Presidential motorcade from here?"

Lori replies, "sure I will be back tomorrow, and as far the motorcade, it's not that important. I can watch it on the five o'clock news."

So, Lori hurries to the stairway and she says, " okay you guys I'm on my way out, I will see if there is a back door to this place and sneak out the back!"

About that time John comes over the radio and says, " I'm moving the camera now; I was scanning the crowd and was looking for some strange activity."

So as Lori, who is rushing towards the building located beside the school book depository, John is trying to zoom in with the camcorder on the second floor of the Dal-Tex building. About that time John replies, " Fredrick you are right, that window is the only window opened on that floor, and as a matter of fact there are two men doing something and they appear to be wearing a painter's uniforms." Lori who is breathing very hard from the trip down the stairs replies, "Okay you guys I'm headed that way!"

About that time Bill who is station several blocks up on Houston street replies, " you guys better get a move on; the motorcade is only a mile from me. I can hear and see the reaction of the crowd. As a matter of fact, there are three Police officers on motorcycles leading the motorcade!"

Bill who is zooming in on the suspicious windows, swings the camera down Houston Street, and replies, "I see them, you guys need to move fast, they are headed this way."

Maggie wait till you hear Bill give you the signal." Within minutes Lori is headed towards the old building, she comes to a side entrance and she notices a truck parked near the door that has the following decal on it, *Joe's Paint and Restoring Service.*

Lori says, "John their truck is parked next to the side entrance, it is a painter's truck!"

Dale who has been sitting quietly on the grassy knoll replies, "

John do you think I should go over there and help Lori?"

John replies "No Dale stay put, we don't have enough time, plus the crowd will only slow you down!"

Dale replies, "okay John but Lori if you need me let me know and I will be there in a flash."

John swings the camera back to the second story window and this time he sees the two men assembling something that appears to be a rifle.

John yells at Lori in the mike, " Lori be careful

they have a gun!" " It looks like a military style rifle!"

Lori who has just reached the top of the stairs screeches to a sudden stop and says, "okay."
But she has to stop and catch her breath, then she says, "okay I can see them, it looks like both of them has rifles, as a matter of fact they do have on uniforms."

John comes over the radio and screams, " Lori get the heck out of there, it's too dangerous!"

But Lori who wants to see more replies, " take it easy John, I am pretty well hidden, and there is too much noise coming from the crowd on Houston Street, it will muffle my voice. Let me stay just a few more minutes and I will sneak back down and leave this place!"

Suddenly Maggie who is parked on the side of the street sees a police officer headed her way, Maggie replies, " John I have trouble, I'm being approached by a police officer hold on, he is signaling for me to roll down the window!"

The police officer walks up to van window and says, " Miss I going to have to ask you to leave this area, the motorcade is fixing to turn here."

Maggie replies, " but officer I won't bother anything, I have the best seat in the plaza, I want to see the president!"

The officer with a mean snarl replies, " lady you will have to exit the car if you want to see the president!"

John replies, "Maggie do what he says, we can't have any trouble, not now anyway!"

So, Maggie prepares to get out of the car and she forgets to turn the van's ignition off when the policeman replies, " and that means turn your van off too!"

So, Maggie the only hope for saving the president turns the ignition off and gets out of the car. So now the team is faced with the dreaded decision of not being able to stop the turn of the motorcade onto Elm Street which will take the limousine

through Dealey Plaza.

Chapter Eight

The team unable to change the motorcade is faced with the dreaded task of watching the horrendous act. About that time Bill comes over the radio and says in a solemn voice, " you guys for what it is worth the motorcade is almost there it is only twenty feet away."

The sound of a policeman's motorcycle muffles in the background, John who is watching the second story window swings the camera towards the Intersection of Houston and Elm street, and he sees the motorcade slowing as it prepares for the turn. The three police motorcycles slow as they swing their motorcycles towards the killing field ahead.

When John replies, " well here we go, we might not be able to stop it, but at least we will have it on camera!"

John takes the camcorder and follows the limousine as it turns onto Houston Street and it heads for Dealey Plaza. John who has sweat running down his brow exclaims, " I'm going to zoom out and try to get that second-floor window into the view finder, so if there is a shot from there I will have in on the camcorder!"

The Limousine slows as it prepares to turn on Elm Street, when John exclaims, " here we go, and there is no turning back now!"

Within seconds Fredrick who is located in the park in front of the grassy knolls starts taking pictures as fast as the camera will shoot. Fredrick who is watching the deadly turn replies, " okay you guys here it comes!"

Lori who is watching the two men over in the Dal-Tex building runs towards the nearest window and says with a whisper, " I'm right beside them, and I'm ready!"

The motorcade slows and heads towards Dealey Plaza, when all of a sudden Fredrick screams, " Lori they are preparing to shoot, I see the barrels hanging out the window!"

Lori who was watching the motorcade turns towards the sniper's nest and says, "my God they are going to shoot!"

Then John who has the whole area in his viewfinder takes the camcorder and zooms in on the sniper's nest and says, "go ahead you guys I can see your faces now!"

About that time the sniper rips off the first shot "*thoom*" and Fredrick screams, " the president has been hit, it looks it's the shot that enters his back and exits from his throat. He has grabbed his throat!"

About that time John has the camera pointed straight into the sniper's nest sees the snipers loading and firing the deadly shots. When there is another shot, "*thoom*" Fredrick who is directly in front of the limousine screams, " I think he missed,

no wait a minute he just shot Connolly!"

When another shot rings out, "***thoom***" about that

time a piece of gravel from the road below

ricochets and hits the bystander located near the

overpass. "***thoom***" another shot rings out and

appears to miss when Fredrick says, " two shots

have hit, and two shots missed!"

About that time Fredrick who is laying on the

ground near the limousine screams," Man this is

unbelievable, they are shooting all around me;

there is dirt and debris flying everywhere!"

 "***thoom***" another shot rings out, this time a shell

fragment skips along the road below, and skips off

the side of the road below where John is located near the overpass. Then John hears a tremendous "***BOOM***" from beside him located behind the picket fence on the grassy knoll. At that time John witnesses, the horrific shot to the head, it enters above the right temple and exits towards the top of the head. John exclaims, "my god that shot came from the grassy knoll!"

Dale who turns and looks toward John exclaims, " I see the smoke from the muzzle, I'm headed that way!"

John follows the limousine as it vanishes under the overpass, and clear out of sight. Then Fredrick who is getting up off the ground explains, " the limousine sped away too fast, I didn't get a chance to do anything!"

About that time the two men located in the Dal-Tex building grabs their gear and down the hall they go, and Lori ducks behind some old furniture as the men race towards the stairs. Lori who is sweating fiercely replies, " boy that was close!"

Lori gets up off the floor and she goes to the window and she sees the men loading up the paint truck and they crank up the truck and out of sight they go. Lori comes over the radio and says, " I'm headed towards the grassy knoll!"

When she runs down the stairs and heads behind the school book depository and to the grassy knoll.

John who is running to find the other sniper under the overpass replies, " Dale he is wearing a policeman uniform, and I think he is headed underneath the overpass."

Dale who has to dodge the spectators replies, " I'm not going to make it, there are too many people around here to dodge!" Lori who is running behind the picket fence replies, " I'm almost there, there is no traffic where I'm at."

Lori continues to run heading towards the overpass, and when she happens to cross Dale who is running towards John replies, " he is underneath, he is wearing a policeman's uniform!" Lori and John heads towards the underpass and when they get there, they see a spent shell and it appears that the man hole cover located beside the cement column is partly open.

John replies, " he is underneath the roadway, he went down a man hole cover!"

Lori reaches down and slides the cover back and peeks down the hole and replies, " I think it is headed towards that restaurant that we stopped at and ate our breakfast!"

About that time Dale and Fredrick walks up and Dale replies, " well we got it on film, but it looks like the snipers got away." John replies, yep and with this traffic we will never make it over there to the restaurant."

Chapter Nine

The team who has failed to capture the assassins, but managed to get the whole thing on tape, is sitting on the curb resting, alongside the roadway located near the grassy knoll. When Bill comes over the radio and says, " hey you guys where are you at?"

John replies, "we are sitting here trying to catch our breath. We will meet you back at the restaurant in just a few minutes!"

Bill replies, "okay we will meet you there."

Bill and Maggie get the van moving and heads towards the restaurant, where the team met for breakfast. Lori who is near exhaustion, appears to weep softly as John notices it and says; "you guys you knew from the start that our chances were pretty slim. Also, we had to be careful because we didn't want to alter history either. But just remember that we weren't supposed to be here anyway. We must gather our thoughts, put aside the emotions and get on with our lives!"

Lori who holds back another tear replies, " well I hated that we couldn't do anything, we had our chance, and we blew it

Furthermore, we should have gone to the police with our story!"

Fredrick speaks up and says, "well we didn't know if they were involved or not. We also couldn't tell anyone because we weren't supposed to be here to begin with. I just look at this whole situation as a near miss that's all!"

Dale who has been quiet speaks up and says, "you know the worse thing about the whole story is we have everything on tape."

Lori replies, "what do you mean the worse thing is we have it taped?"

Dale replies, "well with the technology of 1963, we can't show it to anyone. We don't have a computer; we don't have a television that has audio and video jacks, we haven't got anything to show this video on. But we do know the truth, and maybe someday someone will find it out."

 With those words spoken the team gets up and begins to cross the road and heads towards the restaurant. Meanwhile the Televisions are filled with the story, police are everywhere, and the solemn team who is filled with dreaded thoughts walks towards Bill and Maggie who are sitting in the van near the front entrance of the restaurant. Maggie who appears to be still crying replies "that was the most terrible event that I have ever witnessed."

Bill looks at John and says, "you know a few days ago I thought you guys were pulling my leg, but now you guys are for real!"

John replies, "well I hated that we got you two involved with our problem."

Bill interrupts and says; " well I personally want to thank you because without you telling me, I wouldn't have even been here to begin with, thank you I appreciate the history lesson, and just think I was actually here."

So, the team heads into the restaurant to take a break and get ready to head back towards Odessa. After a very quiet meal the team tips the waitress and pays the tab, and the team gets into the old

Ford van, and down the road they go headed home.

Dale who is riding in the back of the van replies, "

hey you guys don't you think that we should tell

someone. I mean we have all the proof we need.

We have Lori's eyewitness account, we have mine,
John's,

Maggie's, heck we have six eye witnesses!"

When Fredrick interrupts and says, " yea your right

but remember we don't want to change history, we

aren't supposed to be here, remember!"

Dale replies, " well we should at least write this

account down on paper and give it to an

investigator at the police department." Lori replies,

" Dale you know we can't do that, if we do then we

will have to explain how we knew it was going to

happen, and why we all were in the right place at the right time, doesn't that sound weird? As far as I'm concerned, this trip is over, there isn't anything we can do to change it, no one is going to believe us."

John replies "I agree with Lori, we can't prove who we are, we are just stuck, we are eyewitnesses of a crime scene, but we can't offer our accounts of today's events."

 Bill who looks back into the rear-view mirror says, " you guys just take it easy, we will stop in about an hour or so and get some rest, we all have done enough today, enough to last me a lifetime."

Chapter Ten

The team begins to leave the city of Dallas when Bill who has been driving for some time says, "if anyone wants to relieve me from driving you can speak up at any time?"

Dale replies, "sure Bill, pull over and let me drive!" Bill find an area to pulls over, and Dale relieves Bill in the driver's seat. Dale who is driving in Texas for the first time says, "which way do I need to take to get back to Abilene"

Bill replies, "just stay on Interstate 80 till you get to Abilene, then once in Abilene take Interstate 20 to Odessa."

Dale settles in for the long ride back to Odessa when he exclaims, "if you guys want me to I will drive the rest of the way, there is no since us staying at a motel, when I can drive a few extra hours and make it home!"

Bill who is riding in the back exclaims, "that's fine with me, but you know what? I hate back seat drivers!"

Suddenly the whole team begins to laugh out loud when Lori says chuckling, "that's the funniest thing I have heard or saw all day!" After a few miles down the road, Dale begins to fumble with the radio dial, and starts searching for a music station. After running through half the dial, he finally finds some soft music for the trip back home. The van which begins to sway to the sound of the music, causes the team to be rocked fast asleep. Dale who is rethinking the day's events, when he begins to slowly drift back to Dealey Plaza. Forgetting that he is taken the team back to Odessa the van begins to sway as it edges towards the side of the road. Finally, he realizes the noise, and he edges the van back to his side of the road. Dale shakes his head to clear the day's thoughts; he cracks the window so the cool evening's breeze blows through his hair helping him to maintain his concentration of the road. The music takes him back to those days in Nashville when he was a teenager. Dale was born and raised in the Music City, and as a young boy of the sixties, he is seemly at home with the time frame he is in. The rest of the team sleeps quietly as if they were at home in bed. As he watches the lines pass before him, he wonders what he is doing as a young boy back in Nashville. He remembers the dreadful day when he heard over the radio of the announcement that the president had been shot. He was in school, and he heard the bad news from his mother when he arrived at home from school. He looks ahead and notices that the sun is beginning to set. He goes back to that time and remembers himself walking home from a friend's house, when he noticed that same sun setting across town. He remembers the orange glow covered the whole sky. He remembers his mother yelling for him because they always had supper around that same time. His parents were the types that never deviated from their routine, and the routine was set as a clock set with time. Within minutes a flash catches him from the corner of his eye, a large truck appears to be in trouble. The large truck begins to cross the yellow line and appears to be within inches of hitting the van. Dale screams, "hold on you guys, we are going to be hit." Dale in a last-ditch effort jerks the wheel, and the van goes flying through the air. It hits a pasture fence and in front of him is a huge oak tree. The van within seconds smacks the huge oak tree and Dale and John is ejected and the van explodes into flames. The fireball rises like a huge cloud in the sky. Smoke billows black and the smell of flesh stenches the air. About that time a man in a pickup truck comes upon the wreckage, he pulls over to try to offer his help. The man runs towards the wreckage, but because of the fire and flame is so intense there is nothing he can do. After about ten minutes had passes a fire truck and ambulance arrived, but they notice that they too have arrived too late. The firemen begin to battle the stubborn blaze which has consumed much of the wrecked van. As the smoke clears the firemen begin to walk towards the wreckage, and as they get closer they notice two bodies, which appears to be ejected from the mangled wreck. As they reach the two victims they notice that they didn't survive the wreckage either. The rescue squad covers the bodies with white sheets as they wait for the arrival of the coroner who will pronounce them dead. About that time a highway patrolman pulls up, and he gets out of his vehicle and walks up to the fireman and begins to ask questions about the wreckage. His name is Tom Loveton, a highway patrolman from Abilene. The fireman begins pointing to the man who was driving the truck, and replies, "there is the man who was drinking and driving the truck, which caused the van to swerve and hit the tree."

Tom looks over at the driver and says, "What happened here?"

The man in a frail voice says, "officer I was coming from Abilene when my truck ran over something in the road. About that time my tire blew out, and I lost control when the van came around the curve and I forced him off the road."

Tom replies, "is there anyone else around here that saw this wreck?"

The officer looks around and no one says a word. The officer walks up to the wreckage and looks to see if there is a tag number on the charred vehicle.

About that time a fireman yells, "over here, I see something lying on the ground!"

Chapter Eleven

As the officer walks over, he sees what looks appears to be a movie camera. And to the left of one of the victims he sees another item that appears to be a Polaroid camera. But the two cameras are a lot different that the cameras of that day. It was compacted in size and appeared to be something out of a science fiction novel. As the officer picks up the two items, he sees something that resembles a book, but because of the intense fire, it's a stack of burnt paper. So, the coroner finally arrives, and he asks the officer "Tom what do we have here"

Tom replies, "looks like the truck over there had a tire to blow out and he forced this van off the road and the van hit this oak tree and burst into flames."

The coroner replies, "well let's get the victim out of the wreckage!"

The coroner along with the rescue squad members start recovering the bodies where they will be taken down to the county morgue where the painstaking task of identifying them will take place. The van's license plate is found in the rubble, and the officer walks to his car and picks up the mike and calls in the license plate number. Tom replies, "central this is car 24, I need you to run the following Texas license plate number V as in Victor R as in Roger 351."

The dispatcher comes back and says, "that number is registered to a Bill Davis who lives at Route Six Box 45 Miller Farm Road Odessa Texas. The vehicle is a 1962 Ford Van, blue in color."

So, after a moment of silence Tom replies, "would you contact the police department in Odessa and see if they can find a next of kin! Also tell them that we will need someone to identify him."

Tom walks over to the coroner and replies, "Calvin looks like we have a make on that van, looks like we have a whole family here. The guy is from Odessa, his name is Bill Davis."

So, the coroner who has recovered all the bodies, places them in a body bags, and loads them into the Ambulance where they will be taken to the morgue. After the officer fills out the paper work, and he arrests the truck driver, the rescue squad, fire department, and coroner heads back to town. As Tom returns to the police department he begins to look at the new evidence and tries to figure out exactly what he has. About that time an officer by the name of Roy walks by and Tom says, "hey Roy you have a minute? I got something I need you to look at!"

Roy walks up and says, "Tom what have you got?"

Tom replies, "I'm not really sure, but it appears to be some kind of camera. But it is very compacted in size, and there appears to be no tape. This other device looks like a camera, but when I opened it up, it didn't have any film only this disk."

Roy replies "maybe it's some kind of prop that is used in a movie, hell we have had all kinds of weird stuff found when I worked in Hollywood."

Tom who completely puzzled replies, "yea I guess you are right!"

Tom takes the two cameras and tags them as evidence, and he carries the items to the storage area where they are locked away as evidence.

Chapter Twelve

The next morning Tom arrives at the police station and he goes to the operator and says, "have you received any calls for me from Odessa?"

The operator replies, "nope sure haven't are you expecting some?"

Tom replies "yep, we had a traffic accident last night, a man and his family were killed and we are expecting to hear from the Odessa police department about the next of kin."

Tom finishes up his paper work and after the shift meeting Tom leaves for the crash scene, he wants to look around some more since it was so dark last night. So, after arriving back at the crime scene, he notices the trail that the van took right before it hit the huge tree. He then walks around the wreckage, he notices that there was a pile of what looked like blue clothing laying among the wreckage. He reaches down and finds that the blue material appears to be some type of uniform. The material appeared to be made of cotton, but what seemed odd was there appeared to be some type of patch or emblem attached to the blue material. But the name on the patch didn't ring a bell. The word on the patch was *"Prospect"* but the rest of the patch was burnt. He also noticed that the pile of ashes might have been several pairs of the same type uniform, thrown together, that was the only thing that he found. He gets on the radio and calls the dispatcher and asked for a wrecker so that the wreckage could be taken back to town. On his way back towards town, the dispatcher comes over the radio and says, "Tom you have a call from Odessa, I think it is about the wreck last evening."

Tom replies "did they leave a number?"

The dispatcher says, "yep but I don't think it will lead anywhere!"

Tom replies "why?"

The dispatcher says, "because it's the number to the Odessa police department, I hate to be the one to tell you, but there is no next of kin! It appears that he and his wife was the only ones in the family."

Tom replies, "well if that is so who are the other four bodies we found in the wreckage?"

The dispatcher replies, "who knows, maybe they were hitchhikers!

Tom hurries back to the police station and runs to the phone and calls the number of the Odessa Police department. The voice on the other end says, "Odessa police department may I help you?

Tom replies, "yes you can this is Sergeant Tom Loveton and I'm with the Abilene Highway patrol, we had a Bill Davis that was involved in a wreck and it appears that his whole family was killed last night. Do you know anything about this family?"

The voice on the other end replied, "could you hold a minute, I will put you through to Sergeant Malone, he will answer your questions!"

So, after a few minutes a man replies, "this is Sergeant John Malone, how can I help you?"

Tom replies "John this is Tom Loveton with the Abilene Highway Patrol, we had a Bill Davis that was killed last night in a traffic accident, do you know him?"

John replied "yep-sure do, he was an auto mechanic and ran a small garage here in Odessa."

Tom replied, "well his whole family was killed last night, do you know who the next of kin might be?"

John replies, "Tom I'm sorry, but there is no next of kin, it appears that him and Maggie didn't have

134

any children. I think he has a brother but I really don't know where he might live!"

Tom replies, "well it appears that there were several passengers in the van with them, but we haven't been able to find any identification on them. It appears to be a total of six passengers, one man, and one woman both in their late fifties. The other passengers were three men, two of them appears to be in their late forties, and one to be in his thirties, and one woman who was in her late twenties."

John replied, "well the two older passengers were probably Bill and Maggie Davis, but I haven't any idea, who the other passenger were."

Tom replies, "well I guess I will ship Bill and Maggie back to Odessa, and we will keep the other passengers here at Abilene. Maybe they were hitchhikers who they had picked up and gave them a lift."

John replies, "let me check around town and see if anyone might be missing. Sometimes Bill and Maggie would travel with some of their old friends, so I will see if that might be the case."

Tom replies, "well good luck because I sure hate to bury these folks as unknowns. I will check with the state and see if they have any missing people. I appreciate you help and good luck in your search."

John replies "same to you, good luck!"

Chapter Thirteen

Tom is relieved that at least two of the victims has been identified. But the mystery that still hasn't been explained the other four who were riding in the van. Tom decided that he would go over to Calvin who works at the county morgue and see if he had found out anything about the mysterious hitchhikers. Tom arrived at the county morgue once inside he noticed that Calvin and his associates were in the examination room looking over his mysterious hitchhikers. Calvin who sees Tom head towards the examination room replied,

"I was going to call you, you will never believe what we have found. The girl that was found in the wreckage has some unusual dental work."

Calvin takes Tom over to the x-ray screen and says, "you see that right molar, look at the type of filling she has, and I have never seen anything like it. Also, she has another one of those fillings located in the back-jaw tooth too. It appears that those fillings are of a substance that is not used today. Also, in the male we will call number two, he has one located on the left bicuspid, either they had the same dentist, or either they came from the same area." Tom replies "well what do you make of it?

Calvin replies, "I'm not sure it must be something new, because where else would they have received something like this?"

Calvin who looked puzzled replied, "I have one of my orderlies checking on it now, so maybe he will come up with something shortly. Besides that, the only thing we have found is one of the men we call number one, has had a pin placed in his ankle, it looks like he has broken his ankle before, I would say at an early age."

Tom says "well I found out who the older couple is, they are Bill and Maggie Davis from Odessa Texas. It appears that Bill was an auto mechanic and the police in Odessa said that he doesn't believe that they had any children. He mentions a brother that he thought Bill had, but he wasn't sure where he might be located."

Calvin replies "are they coming after the bodies, are we going to need to deliver them?"

Tom replies "well we don't know at the moment what's going to happen, they are supposed to call me back. But if I had to make a guess, we will probably have to ship them ourselves!"

Tom leaves the county morgue and heads back to the police station where he plans to check out some other leads on the supposed hitchhikers. As Tom heads back towards the police station, he stops at a country store located just outside of town. Tom who knows the owner asks the clerk if he has seen anyone pass through the area that looked out of place?"

The clerk, whose name is Alvin replies, "you know now that you mentioned it, I do remember a van load of folks stopping by here about two days ago. They were acting funny; it appears that they were fascinated about the prices, and the stuff I had hanging on the wall. One of them asked me about the Harry Truman autograph there on the wall. He also said something about my store looked like a picture out of the history books. There was some kind of discussion about the price of gas, something about paying 1.85 a gallon somewhere."

Tom interrupts the man and says; "do you remember how many people they were? Do you remember what kind of car they were driving?" Alvin replied "they weren't in a car, they were in a blue Ford Van, as best as I can remember there were two women and four men. What was funny about them was that some of them were wearing blue uniforms, something that a pilot would wear! I also noticed that the uniform had a patch which read prospector, and what stuck out the most was it appeared to be some kind of space craft on it!" Tom who was complete surprises says, "prospector? What in the world is a prospector doing with a flight suit on?"

Alvin replied "you got me, because I went home and looked up the name, that is why I remember it so."

Tom replies, "was there anything else you remember about them?"

Alvin replies, "one of the men was carrying a camera, or something that looked like a camera, but this thing was different. You know that when you take a picture of something, the camera has to be rewound with a handle, well this thing appears to rewind itself. He was snapping pictures of everything, pictures on the walls, he even took a picture of my cash register! It seemed odd at the time but nothing surprises me these days!"

Tom who looked dumbfounded replies, "yep I know what you mean, and I saw the camera too, it was found in the wreckage. It appears that they all died in that crash we had last night." Alvin who looked upset replied, "well they sure were nice folks, I will never forget those folks as long as I live. They really made me proud of my store!"

Chapter Fourteen

Tom leaves the store with the new information. But what troubled him the most was why were they headed to Abilene from Odessa? And where did they pick the hitchhikers up at? And why were they wearing blue flight suits? After a few miles down the road, Tom reached over and turns on the radio. And the announcer was talking about the assassination of John F Kennedy. Then suddenly in dawned on Tom why the van was traveling through Abilene. The van must have been coming from Dallas, and that might explain the cameras. Tom rushes back towards the police department to check out the camera's that he had found in the wreckage Within minutes he arrives, and he goes running to the evidence room, where the cameras are located. He picks up the cameras, and he goes back to his desk to inspect the evidence from the wreckage. As he holds up the digital camera to the light, he accidentally hits the button and the flash lights up the room. Everyone in the office jumps up and they come running over to see what all the commotion is all about. One of the officers exclaims, "what in the world was that all about?"

Tom replies, "well I stopped at the old country store located just outside of town. There I spoke to the owner named Alvin, according to him the van stopped there in a few days ago. He told me all about the vanload of tourist, and I think they were headed towards Dallas! Alvin said that one of the men had a camera, and that he was taking pictures of everything in the store. I rushed back here to see if he was right, and you know what? This thing here is a high-tech camera, and they used this camera to take pictures of the presidents visiting Dallas! And I bet that this other thing here is a movie camera. So now I know I have just about figured out the reason why Bill and Maggie Davis were doing here in Abilene. I also know what these two items are, and who they were taking pictures of, but I still don't know who the people were in the blue flight suits!"

Tom takes out the movie camera, and he tries to figure out how the thing works. He takes off the covers that are covering the lens, he finds the switch and to his surprise the camera comes on, then as soon as it came on, it went back off. Tom who looks dumbfounded replies; "well it worked for a second, but now it has gone back off. I guess it must have gotten broken when it was thrown from the vehicle."

Tom decides that he will take the two cameras down to the local television repair shop. There is a friend of his that works on all the latest televisions, and radios in the town. Tom arrives at the television shop and he walks in he sees Phil the manager standing near the counter. Tom approaches the counter and Phil replies, "what can I help you with today Tom?" Tom replies, "well I picked up these two items at a wreck we had late last night. I was wondering if you would look at them and tell me how they work. I think this big one is a movie camera, and the small one is a camera used to take still photographs!"

Phil replies, "well let me see what we have here!" Phil takes the movie camera out and begins to examine it and he looks over at Tom and says, "well I can tell you one thing, I've never seen anything like it before, but it does appear to be a camera, but I've never seen one this compacted before. Also, I've never seen one that doesn't have an electrical cord attached to it. Look at the design, it appears to be made to fit in a man's hand. I can't believe how light it is, usually these things weight several hundred pounds."

Tom looks over at him and says, "see if you can turn that thing on. I saw a small switch there on the left, but when I turned on the switch, it came on for a second, and then it went back off."

Phil who still looks confused replies, "Tom I don't have any idea how this thing works, but if you want too, leave it with me and let me take it apart, and see if I can figure this thing out." Tom replies, "I'm sorry Phil, but these two items are all the evidence that I have of the crime scene, I can't leave them here. But if you want to, you can come by the station later and we can work on them there!"

Phil replies, "okay we can do that, I will be there around 5pm or so."

Tom looks at Phil and says, "okay sounds good, I will see you then!"

Tom leaves the repair shop and heads back to the station to takes the two cameras back to the evidence room where he locks them backup until

Phil arrives at five o'clock.

Chapter Fifteen

Phil arrives at the police station to take a look at the cameras. He has brought a host of tools with him, in which he hopes to solve the mystery with the highly advanced cameras. So, he walks in to the station and asks the clerk sitting at the desk, "I'm here to see Tom Loveton!"

The clerk replies, "one moment please."

She picks up the phone and rings Tom's desk. Tom, who was finishing up some last-minute paperwork, reaches over and answers the phone. "Hello this is Tom Loveton how may I help you?"

The clerk replies "Tom there is a man to see you." Tom looks at his watch and says, "okay I will be there in a minute!"

Tom walks over to the front desk and says, "Hey Phil come on back!"

So, the two men start walking for the stairs headed for the evidence room. As they are walking Tom looks over at Phil and says, "well maybe we will be able to get that camera running and see what is on that thing."

Phil replies, "well we will give it our best shot, but I'm not sure we have the ability to fix that crazy thing."

Tom and Phil enter the evidence room and they pick up the two cameras and they head over to an empty interrogation room located just a few feet away from the clerk's desk. Phil picks up the movie camera and hold it up to the large light located in the room.

Phil replies "I think that this camera is operated by some sort of onboard power supply. There is a plug located on the rear of the unit and it appears that it might have a plug-in type cord that might provide some power to it. Do you recall seeing any type of electrical cord in the wreckage?"

Tom looks over at Phil and says, "no not that I saw, but the fire was so intense that it probably burned up in the fire from the wreckage!"

Phil replies, "well I guess we are going to have to make one." Phil reaches in his bag of tools and pulls out a plain piece of wire with two clips attached to it. He then pulls out a voltage meter and

checks the voltage on the camera's cord outlet. The

meter shows a voltage of 16 volts, Phil replies,

"well I have a power supply that register 12 volts,

but it won't go up any higher than that. We will try

it anyway, maybe we can get the camera to operate

at that low of a voltage."

Phil attaches the two clips to the camera's plug in and looks at Tom and says, "where is the nearest electrical outlet around here?"

Tom pointing his finger replies, "over there, I will get it"

Tom grabs the electrical cord and walks over and plugs it into the wall outlet. Phil who is beginning to sweat replies, "okay here we go!"

He turns on the power supply and reaches over to

the side of the camera and hits the switch to the

camera. The men notice that the eyepiece of the camera lights up and then it goes back out again. Phil who is determined to fix the camera replies, "I think that the camera has internal damage! Let's look at the inside of it and see what makes this thing tick."

Phil reaches over and turns off the power supply and unclips the wires and he looks at the camera and sees several screws, he reaches over to his toolbox and begins to hunt for a screwdriver that will fit the tiny screws. Tom looks over and says, "who ever built this thing really had a thing for being compacted, I have never seen any screws that tiny before!"

Phil begins to take the screws out one by one when he wipes his brow and says "I'm going to have to get me some Bifocals if everything is going to start having screws this small in them." After about five minutes or so, Phil reaches and grabs the camera and tries to separate the two halves', when the camera comes apart and Phil exclaims, "what in the world do we have here! In all of my days as a television repairman I have never seen anything like this."

Tom leans over and says "what is that green looking panel with the silver streaks on it?" Phil replies, "I have no idea!"

Phil lays one of the halves on the side and begins to examine the camera's components and try to determine what the problem is. After several minutes Phil replies, "Tom I have no idea how this thing works. But I do think that the black box located on the rear of the camera is the battery. Phil points to the label attached to it and says see this label right here, it says something about disposing of this thing properly and there is a corrosive label attached right here. If I pull on this thing it might come off."

So, Phil grabs the end of the black box and lifts up on it and it detaches from the camera and Phil says, "see I told you that thing was a battery, but I have never seen one that was shaped like that before!"

Tom whose eyes are getting wider by the moment exclaims, "Phil who do you think makes such a device? If we have never seen anything like this where did it come from?"

Phil who is completely dumbfounded replies "I have no idea, but if I had to make a bet, I would say that this is some kind of military hardware. Because who would use something like this except the military or maybe someone from Hollywood! And I don't think anyone in Hollywood would be smart enough to come up with something like that!"

The two men erupt in laughter and Tom replies, "I guess we have done all that we can."

Phil replies, "yep I guess you are right, I have no idea how this thing works. I have never been in the military, furthermore I think that I might do more harm than good."

The two men agree that because neither of them has any idea how to fix the camera, they decide to put the thing back together.

After about ten minutes of silence, Tom looks over at Phil and says, "do you want to look at the other camera?"

Phil replies, "I don't think I can do anything with it either, both of those cameras are too advanced for me, remember I'm just a TV repairman."

Tom replies, "you know that these two cameras might have some pictures of the president's visit to Dallas on them. The people that were carrying these cameras were on their way back home from Dallas when they were killed in that terrible wreck we had a few days ago." Phil looks over at Tom and says, "Tom we might not ever know what happened in Dallas, even if we could fix these two things!"

Tom replies, "well I guess I will take these things home once the case is closed, because they aren't doing anybody around here any good. I know that if we can't get these things fixed, I know no one else can!"

Phil replies, "well if you don't take them I want them, if I can't fix them at least they will make good conversation pieces in my living room."

So, after a few minutes of cleaning up the table and putting the two cameras back in the evidence room, the two men leave the police station and get in their cars and heads off towards town. Tom, who is thinking about the cameras as he is driving home, wonders just what is on those two cameras, and how come they couldn't get them working again.

Chapter Sixteen

Early the next morning Tom arrives at the police station and he heads towards his desk to begin another day at the old police station. Tom walks over to the dispatcher and says, "I will be going over to the coroner's office today and see what Calvin has found out on our crash victims. I should be back around lunchtime."

Tom leaves the police station and heads downtown to visit the county morgue. Once he arrives he walks in the coroner's office and he see Calvin sitting at a table drinking a cup of coffee. Tom replies "well anything new on our crash victims?" Calvin replies, "well no nothing worth shouting about, we did find out that the dental work is a new filling that is being widely used in the military. It seems that instead of using silver they have switched to another metal which is a lot stronger than silver. Have you found out anything new?" Tom replies, "no not really, seem the two cameras we found in the wreckage are broken and Phil and I took them apart last night. They are made of electrical components that we have never seen before, it is possible that they are some kind of military cameras."

Calvin replies, "have you contacted the military about those crash victims? If they are military cameras do you think they might be looking for them?"

Tom replies, "well if the crash victims were military personnel don't you think we would have found some kind of identification on them? They would have had dog tags on them don't you think?"

Calvin replies "yep I guess you are right, but it does seem odd that we couldn't identify them!"

Tom replies "well looks like we will never know who they are, and if we don't find out soon we are going to have to bury them as unknowns."

Calvin replies "yep because their bodies are decomposing fast, we need to do something with them. I have completed the autopsies, and as soon as you want too we can go ahead and bury them. I have complete fingerprints, and photos of the deceased so as far as I'm concerned we can bury them."

Tom replies "I will check with the chief and see what he thinks, I will call you later this afternoon." Finally, Tom leaves the county morgue and heads back over to the crash site since he is in the area and take one more look before he closes the case. After arriving at the crash site, he walks the whole crime scene and looks at every detail that comes across his mind. After about 45 minutes of combing the pasture, he decides that he has come to the end of his investigation at the crime scene. He gets in his car and heads to the impound yard to take one last look at the van. After about twenty minutes he enters the impound yard, and he walks over to the crumbed van and takes one last look. He combs over the wreckage and starts walking back towards his police car in an effort to bring closure to this terrible accident. Every time he is around the wreckage he wonders who the mystery passengers are, and wonders how come no one has reported them missing. He then gets into the police cruiser and heads back to the station. As soon as he arrives back at the station, the dispatcher motions for him to come over to his desk, it appears that he has a message for him. Tom replies "what have you got?"

The dispatcher says, "well we have a friend of Bill Davis coming to claim the bodies. He is going to take Bill and Maggie back to Odessa but he wants to leave the other victims here. The sheriff says that no one is missing from Odessa except Bill and Maggie. He should be here around 2pm."

Tom replies "call Calvin over at the morgue and tell him the news about the guy coming to identify Bill and Maggie. Tell him I will be there as soon as they arrive here at the station."

So as Tom prepares for the visitors from Odessa, he begins to finish up his report of the accident. He then goes into the chief's office and takes his report so that the chief can sign off on it. The chief's name is James Smith, a thirty-year veteran of the force, who is a native of Abilene and has worked at the station all of his life.

Tom walks into James's office and says" chief here is the report on that car wreck we had two days ago. A party from Odessa is coming to claim the two Davis family members, but it looks like we will have four unidentified victims left for us to bury. Calvin at the morgue wants to go ahead and bury them because of the condition of the bodies. I think we should go ahead and bury them, we have pictures, fingerprints, and dental records of the victims."

James replies "have you search the missing persons archive in the research room?"

Tom replies, "yep sure did, but nothing that fits our victims, we did find a local country store clerk who saw the tourist, but he has never seen any of them before. We think that the four victims were hitchhiking and Bill picked them up on his way to Dallas."

 James replies "well let's keep searching but go ahead and tell Calvin to prepare them for burial."

Tom replies "will do chief." so, Tom walks out of the chief's office and heads towards his desk and prepares to call the county morgue. Tom calls

Calvin and tells him to prepare the four victims

for burial.

Chapter Seventeen

Around two o'clock two men pulls up in front of the police station in a jet-black hearse. The two men enter the police station and ask the clerk for Tom Loveton. Tom who saw the hearse pulls up, walks in and replies "I'm Tom Loveton and you two guys must be from Odessa?"

The older man replies, "yes, we are, my name is Jake Farmer, and this is my nephew Mike."

Tom tells the two men to follow him to the county morgue and they leave the station and heads out the door. After arriving at the morgue Tom leads the two men into the morgue and introduces them to

Calvin who will fill out the release papers and process the two bodies out. Tom looks over at Jake and says, "I want to thank you two guys for coming out and picking up the bodies, I sure am sorry for us meeting like this, but sometimes things just happen. The only information I have is Bill and Maggie had picked up four hitchhikers, on their way to Dallas. After they left Dallas they were involved in a wreck that included a tractor-trailer. The driver had a tire to blow out, and he swerved to miss the van, but the van swerved off the road and hit an oak tree and exploded on impact. All the passengers perished in the fire."

Jake replies "I'm sorry to hear that Bill had to die like that. He was a very kind man who would help you anyway he can. He ran a garage located just outside Odessa, he has been known to work on a friend's car and sometimes he wouldn't charge them for the service. His wife Maggie was the best cook in town she was a kind woman who was a great woman of the church."

Tom who fights back a tear replies, "you know I fill I know these folks just like they have lived here all their life. If you will follow Calvin he will show you where the remains are and you can fill out the report and you will need to sign some release papers." So, the two men follows Calvin into the morgue where they will pick up the remains. After about ten minutes are so the men come out with the two bodies, and Jake goes and gets the hearse and backs it up to the loading area. The two men then load the remains and then they shut the doors on the hearse, and looks back at Tom with a solemn smile and says, "Tom thanks for you hard work, the town of Odessa welcome you and your family anytime and thanks for taken care of them!"

Tom nods his head and replies "you are very welcome; you guys drive safely and have a nice drive back."

Tom walks over to Calvin and says, "I just wished we could find out who the others are, but I guess we will never know." Tom leaves the morgue and heads back to the police station where he will finish up the paper work and closes the case.

Chapter Eighteen

The next morning the whole police station, and some local residences prepare for a morning service to bury the last victims of the wreck. The service is located at the county graveyard where a local pastor of the local town will conduct the service. The officers acted as pallbearers for the four victims. The county residence had grown attached to the victims and everyone thought of them as members of the local town. The service was a sad occasion, with several residences wiping tears as the local officer lowered the crash victims to their permanent grave. Each victim had a case number inscribed on their simple headstone along with the following inscription, *"here lies four friends who is known only to God, may they rest in internal peace."* After the service, Tom walks over to Calvin and says "Calvin thank you for your hard work and dedication"

Calvin replies "it's time like these that make my job a hard one."

Tom gets into the police car and heads back to do his daily routine as a highway patrolman. Later that afternoon Tom arrives back at the station to process some traffic tickets that he had wrote during his shift. Tom walks into the chief's office and says "James I want to know if it would be all right for me to take those two cameras back home. The case

is pretty much over, and I want to keep those items

for memories' sake."

James replies "I guess so Tom, you were the officer

to find them, and there is no use to us, they are

broken anyway!"

Tom, who is finishing up his shift, turns around and
says "thanks James, you have a good evening and I
will see you in the morning."

Tom walks towards the door and heads for the

stairway which will take him to the evidence room,

he then walks over and asks the clerk for the

cameras. The clerk hands Tom the clipboard and

Tom signs the two items out and says, "maybe

someday we will find out how to fix these things!"

The clerk replies "yep someday soon I hope!"

So, Tom leaves the police station and heads home. On his drive towards his ranch, he can't get the four hitchhikers out of his mind. He tries to image what it would be like to travel down the road with them. He wonders what they looked like, and what their voice might sound like. Soon he turns into the long and winding driveway that heads to his home where he finds his family getting ready for supper. He walks in and with a solemn voice saying "Boy have I had a rough day, I'm ready for some supper!"

His wife and two sons run for the dinner table and Tom walks in and lays the box which contains the two cameras. His youngest son Jason exclaims "what do you have daddy? Is it something for me?" Tom replies "nope Jason I'm sorry."

So as his family sits at the dinner table Tom explains the story behind the mysterious box and the two items that he found in the wreckage. He also goes into all the details about their flight suits, and about the patches he found in the fire. He reminds them that someday hopefully that someone will be able to fix the cameras, and hopefully he will find out what's on them. He reminds his sons to keep themselves fit so that one day they will find out the truth and solve this mystery of the unknown visitors that died that day in the fiery crash.

Chapter Nineteen

Some fifty-four years has passed since Tom has found those cameras in that terrible wreck of 1963. Tom who is in his late seventies, has long since retired and still lives in Abilene. His son Jason has taken his old job as the highway patrolman for the county. Jason is a splitting image of his dear old dad and is on his way to work to start another day in the city of Abilene. Jason arrives at the police station to pick up his police cruiser and gets ready to hit the busy interstates of Abilene. Around 2pm, a Wednesday afternoon he gets a call on the radio about a terrible wreck that has happened near Abilene. He is only a short distance away from it, so he answers the call and down the road he goes on his way to the wreck. He arrives at the scene when to his amazement he noticed it has happen in the same curve that the local town remembers the accident in 1963. Jason runs over to that dreaded oak tree and it appears that another van load of passengers has crashed in the very same spot that the four unknowns perished some fifty-four years ago. Jason who has erased that story from his mind until now when he remembers the story his dad told him that night at the supper table. Jason who can't believe that he had forgotten the old story jumps from the police cruiser and runs towards the wreckage. His friend Ronald works for the rescue squad says "hey Jason do you remember this spot, remember the four unknowns that died here some fifty-four years ago?"

Jason replies "you know I have forgotten all about this place until I came around the curve, then it all came back to me just like it was yesterday!"

Jason goes down to the wreckage and notices that two men were killed and they burned up also from the fiery wreckage. The victim was from Dallas, and the victim appeared to be two salesmen on their way back to Odessa. Jason fills out the accident report, and he heads back towards Abilene to file his report. On his way back, he starts to recall the story that his dear old dad told him some fifty-four years earlier. As he gets closer towards the station he reaches over and turns on the radio and listens to the local news report that the local radio station airs each afternoon. About that time a special report comes over the radio and Jason reaches over and turns up the volume, in order to drown out the police radio. The announcer reports "Today at 2:15 PM the space program has lost its new space shuttled called prospector, it was on its maiden voyage and it disappeared around 2:15pm local time this afternoon. The four-crew members appeared to have been lost in the disaster which is a first since the other shuttle explosion in 1986. More details will be released as soon as the information is made available."

Jason who can't believe what he just heard, reaches for his cell phone to call his dad and tell him of the dreaded news. Tom answers the phone is a solemn voice "hello"

Jason replies "dad have you hear about the crash?"

Tom replies "yes I sure did what about it?"

Remember that car wreck that you had back in 1963?

"Tom replies, "yes I sure do!"

Jason replies, "well the local radio just announced that one of our space shuttles just went missing, and it appears to have been lost."

Tom replies "well what does that have to do with the wreck?" Jason replies "the name of it is prospector, now does that ring a bell!"

Tom who is completely dumbfounded replies "you have got to be kidding me, there is no way that this could be happening!"

Jason replies "yes I'm afraid so, do you still have those cameras?"

Tom replies "yes I sure do, and that box hasn't been opened in over fifty-four years."

Jason replies "well get that box out and I will pick you up at six o'clock."

Tom replies "okay sounds good I will be ready when you get here."

Chapter Twenty

So, Jason rushed to his father's house after work. When Jason arrives at his father's house he notices his dad sitting on the front porch with that box sitting in his lap. Jason replies "how long have you been waiting dad?"

Tom replies "about two hours I guess, but that's okay, I've been sitting here thinking about that wreck which happed so long ago. Do you think we can get it to work?"

Jason replies "I'm pretty sure we can, it's been fifty-four years, and with the latest technology we have I'm sure someone can fix it. You know dad I've never seen those cameras."

Tom replies "you got to be kidding me not once?"

Jason replied "nope never did, I figured that it was very important to you, and I figured that it was best if I left it alone." Tom replies "well it's been such a long time, I can't remember them myself."

Jason replies "well we will both see them in about two minutes!" Jason arrives at his house and his wife is fixing supper. Jason says "honey we will be out in the garage for a little while, put the supper in the stove we will eat later. We have something very important to work on."

His wife exclaims "well don't take too long, or your supper will get cold."

Jason and his dad heads for the garage, once there the two men begin to clear off the work table and Tom places the box on the table. Jason reaches over and when he takes the lid off Jason exclaims "dad do you know what you have?

It's a camcorder, and that there is a digital camera, you have got to be kidding me, you have had these two cameras all this time?"

Tom replies "yep over fifty-four years, and I never was able to get them to work!"

Jason replies "no wonder there was no such a thing back in 1963. The technology wasn't there yet. I mean we had movie cameras, but we didn't have camcorders and digital cameras. No wonder you couldn't get them to work, the batteries are probably dead on the cameras, let's go upstairs I might have a battery that will fit this thing, if not I'm sure we can buy one."

So, Jason grabs the cameras and off towards the house they go.

When Jason replies "there is no one that will believe this story. How in the heck did these cameras wind up in Abilene?"

Tom replies "remember that story I told you fifty-four years ago? I told you that there were four people who died in a bad wreck and we couldn't identify them. Well those two cameras came from the wreckage."

Jason who is shaking from excitement yells, "well we are fixing to find out what is on the tape. Dad, we have had these type cameras for almost 20 years now. How come you never recognized these things on TV, or in the papers, I see these things every day."

Tom replies "I guess I have blocked it out of my mind, that day was a very painful time in my life. And since I couldn't ever identify the victims, I sort of blackout the disappointing details of that dreadful day. A man has to forget something's and move on with his life, and that is what I decided to do."

So, Jason and Tom reach the spare bedroom and he takes the battery off the camera and reaches for his camera in the closet. He takes the battery off his camera and to their surprise it fits as if it was made for it. Jason grabs the camera, along with the audio and Video adapter cord from his camera, and over to the television they go. Jason plugs in the cord and turns on the camera and behold the camera comes on and it is working as if it's never been turned off before. When Tom exclaims, "how did you do that so easy? We never could get it to come on and stay on, it would only run for a few seconds!"

Jason replies "well dad if the battery is dead, that is exactly what the camera will do!"

Jason reaches over and he hit's the rewind button and the camera begins to moan and whiz when Tom yells, "what in the heck is it doing now?"

Jason replies "I'm rewinding the tape, there is a tape located inside of the camera. The camera records and the tape copies what the camera is being pointed at. Once the tape stops, we will get to see what is on the tape."

Jason who is amazed at what his father has found sits in anticipation of what the tape is fixing to show after nearly fifty-four years, the truth is about to be known. Tom who is filled with excitement exclaims, "when is that stupid thing going to stop?"

Jason replies "it must have a lot on it because it

sure is taking a long time for it to rewind!"

About that time the camera comes to a screeching

stop and Jason looks at his dad, and his dad looks

at Jason, and Jason says in a loud voice "okay here

we go!"

Chapter Twenty-one

After fifty-four years of complete silence,

Jason hits the play button, and the camera comes to

life. Jason and his dad are glued to the television

set as the tape begins to appear on the TV. About

that time Tom's fifty-four years of wondering have

finally come to an end. The tape begins with a

picture of John Snow introducing the crew and he

names everyone and he goes into details about their

mission. Tom interrupts and says; "that must be the

unknowns buried in the county cemetery, look they

are wearing their blue flight suits!"

The shuttle captain continues to talk about their mission and describes in full detail the purpose of their mission. Jason who is in complete awl replies "my God, it is the prospector crew! And look there is a picture of the shuttle, my God dad this is unbelievable!" As the tape continues to rolls, the crew is described in detail and mentioned by name. Suddenly there is a few seconds pause, and the tape begins again. This time it shows a small farm house that is surrounded by old cars. "That must be Bill's and Maggie's house," exclaims Tom.

Then the camera skips and then it begins again but this time it is showing Dealey Plaza and the surrounding area located in Dallas Texas. Jason interrupts and says "where is that footage coming from!"

About that time the tape continues, and it shows the motorcade that John F Kennedy is riding in. Tom who is glued to the set exclaims "I knew it, I knew it all along" Jason looks at his dad and says, "what are you talking about?"

Tom exclaims "it's the John F Kennedy assassination, I always knew that that camera had that on it. Because that would have been the only reason that Bill and Maggie would have gone to Dallas for and that was to see the president!"

Jason continues to watch the tape in amazement replies, "this tape shows everything!"

About that time, he reaches for the volume control and he turns the sound up as he prepares to watch the president ambushed motorcade. The tape continues as John voice narrates the tape, also in the background they hear a discussion of Lee Harvey Oswald's moves, and about the men in the Dal-Tex building. Jason Interrupts and says "my God they are telling the whole story as it happens." Soon they hear the last shot and notices that John was zooming in on the head shot. Then they hear the discussion about the sniper at the grassy knoll, they also noticed the snipers faces in the Dal-Tex building. After a few seconds the tape shuts off and the two men sit there in complete silence. Jason who is holding back a tear exclaims "my God dad we just witnessed the complete ambush of John F

Kennedy. We actually saw the whole thing, from front to the ending. This is unbelievable!"

Tom who is wiping a tear exclaims, "I always knew that it had something important about the John F Kennedy assassination." Jason replies "I wonder who else knows about this tape, I bet if the CIA and the FBI knew we had this we would be in trouble. There are a lot of people in the world would kill for this information as a matter of fact they probably wouldn't believe what we just saw." Jason looks at his dad and says "you know what? I bet that other camera might have some more to it, hold on and let me go get it." Tom replies "heck bring the whole box, it has all of my reports and files on that case." Jason runs down stairs and

heads for the garage to bring the whole box back

upstairs.

Chapter Twenty-two

Jason returns to the upstairs bedroom with the box that his father kept for fifty-four years. Jason reaches inside and pulls out the digital camera and opens a side compartment and pulls the small disk out of the camera. Tom replies "yep I have seen that before, but how does it work?"

Jason replies "this here is a compact flash card, better known as memory disk. It is a disk used to store information on it. These pictures from the camera are stored digitally on it."

Jason reaches over and turns his computer on and the computer comes to life. After three or four minutes has passed Jason slams the disk in the computer, and he exclaims, "watch this dad!" Jason opens up the file manager and click on picture number one. It shows pictures of someone house, and farm, along with a picture of cars and trucks. About that time Tom replies "that must be Bill and Maggie's house, the policemen from Odessa said that Bill ran a garage in Odessa." Jason continues to click on each picture as Tom gives out the details. Tom replies "that's the old country store that I used to get gas at, and look there is the old cash register that the old man told me about. And look that is a picture of the school book depository, and that's a picture of the sniper's nest, and that is a picture of the snipers."

About that time Jason says, "look at that one right there, it is a picture of the president's head being blown off!"

Jason who is in a dazed state replies "dad I can't believe that you have had these pictures for fifty-four years. They appear to look as if they were taken yesterday, this is unbelievable, I'm speechless!" Tom who is smiling proudly replies "well I always knew that those cameras were special, I just didn't know how important until now. What should we do with this new information now that we have seen it!"

Jason replies "Dad we have to contact NASA, they need to know, that we have found the crew!"

Tom replies "I guess you are right, but what about the contents of the cameras, and the camcorders details of the assassination footage?"

Jason replies, "what about it?"

Tom replies, "You know how the government works, they won't believe our story, and they will file the evidence away, and we will never know the truth, about that dreadful day!"

Jason replies, "I can make copies of all this information before we hand it over to them!"

Tom replies, "now that is a good idea! You start copying the files, and I will call NASA, and by the way, make sure you get the part of John talking about the crew, and then delete everything else after that!"

Jason replies, "Consider it done!"

 Jason takes the memory cards out of the camera, and puts it in his computer, and begins copying the pictures to his thumb drive. He then takes the camcorder memory tape and opens it up into his video editing software. He makes a copy of the file, leaving the first part alone, and then deletes everything that happened in Dealey plaza. So now all that is left on the tape is John introducing the crew, and the video, taken at Bill Davis's house.

Jason looks over to his dad and replies, "dad everything is deleted and copied over to my thumb drive, I left all the pictures on the camera, except what they took at Dealey plaza, and edited the video tape."

Tom with a large grin on his face replies, "let's call NASA, and we will show them what we have, and then we will go from there!

Jason takes out his cell phone and Google's the phone number of NASA's headquarters. He clicks on the number, and after a few rings, a lady answers the phone and says, "hello, NASA spaceflight center, how may I help you today?"

Jason replies, "my name is Jason Loveton, I'm a highway patrolman with the Abilene highway patrol, I think, I know where your space shuttle crew, "prospector" is located!"

The lady replies, "hold on, I need to transfer you to the local accident investigation team located in your state, what state are you calling from?"

Jason replies, "Texas, I'm calling from Abilene!"

The lady replies, "my goodness, let me find Mason Anderson, and get him on the phone, he is the project manager for the accident and recovery project team, let me find him, hold on!"

Jason replies, "no problem!

After about two minutes are so, a man on the other end of the line replies, "This is Mason Anderson, how may I help you!"

Jason replies, "my name is Jason Loveton, I'm a highway patrolman with the Abilene highway patrol, I think I know where your space shuttle crew, "prospector" is located!"

Mason replies, "You found the crew?"

Jason replies, "yes sir, they are buried in the county graveyard, been there since 1963!"

Mason replies, "What about the crash site, do you have it secured!"

Jason who is presently surprised by the response replies, "No, but I have several items that belong to this crew, I have suits, patches, camera, and a camcorder! I also have autopsy reports, and dental records!"

Mason replies, "do you know whcre the crash site is, we need the crash site?"

Jason replies, "I do not know where that is located, but I do have police reports from the investigation."

Mason replies, "Where can I meet you and when?"

Jason replies, "how far are you from Abilene?"

Mason says, "currently I'm near Fort Worth, I can be there in about two hours!"

Jason replies, "okay call me at the Abilene police station when you get near Abilene, I'm on duty till 11pm, do you need the address."

Mason replies, "No, I'm using the GPS in my car, I will see you around 7pm."

Jason replies, "okay sounds good!"

Jason hangs up the phone, and looks at his dad and says, "Mason will be here at 7pm, I can't wait to see the look on his face, when he sees what we have!"

Tom replies, "I've been waiting fifty-four years for this, I wouldn't miss this for anything!"

Mason hangs up the phone call from Jason, he thumbs through his contact list, and select another number and waits for an answer. Suddenly a male voice replies, "hello!"

Mason replies, "Mason here, I think I found something, I just had a call and I'm going to check it out!"

The male voice replies, "do you have the wreckage!"

Mason replies, "no, but I think I have found the crew!"

The male voice replies, "We need the wreckage, let me know if you find the wreckage!"

Mason replies, "I will, I'm about two hours away from the call, as soon as I find out something I will call you back."

The male voice replies, "Where are you?"

Mason replies, "Fort Worth, Texas!"

The male voice says, "let me know if we need to send the recovery crew!"

Mason replies, "you will be the first to know!"

Mason hangs up the phone, he gets on Interstate 20 and heads west, he presses down on the gas pedal, and off towards Abilene he goes!

Chapter Twenty-three

Tom and Jason begin to prepare for Mason visit which is only two hours away. Jason looks over towards his dad and replies, "what do you want to make copies of, I know he will take some items back with him?"

Tom replies, "Let's make copies of the autopsy, and dental records, and all of my investigative files!"

Jason replies, "what about the uniforms? Don't you think we need to keep a sample of the uniforms?"

Tom replies, "yes, especially save one of the patches, we want to make sure, that if someone questions our story, we have something to back it up!"

Jason continues to make copies of all the items, he takes out his thumb drive, and copies all the files on it. Then he burns a CD, so they will have a hard copy of everything. He then precedes to box everything up, and him and Tom waits for Mason visit, sometime around 7pm.

Mason who is only a few miles away, reaches for his cellphone, and redials Jason number, the phone begins to ring, when suddenly Jason replies,

"hello."

Mason replies, "Can I speak to Jason Loveton?

This is Mason Anderson!"

Jason replies, "this is Jason!"

Mason replies, "I'm almost there, are you at the

station?"

Jason replies, "yes, me and my dad are here, we

have the evidence!"

Mason replies, "I'm pulling into the parking lot

now, see you in a few!"

Jason replies, "I will meet you at the door!"

Jason and Tom heads to the front door, both men

greet Mason, as the three shakes hands, Jason

replies, "follow us, we have the evidence in room B!"

Jason walks down the narrow hallway and they enter the second room on the left. There in the room, is a television, laptop computer, and the old box, which contains all the evidence. As the men sit down at the table, Jason replies, "Mason my dad was the patrolman on call that night, so I will let him tell you the story!"

Tom stands up and heads to the front of the table, he begins to tell Mason the story about the van crash, he opens up the box, and starts taken the items out, and placing on the table. Mason who can't believe the items that are being placed on the table replies, "how long have you had these items?"

Tom replies, "1963!"

Mason who reaches for the camera replies, "you can buy these things anywhere!"

Tom who is disappointed by Mason reply, looks over at him and says, "here check this out, so he reaches into the box, and pulls out the soiled and torn uniforms, what do you think about this?"

Mason replies, "it looks like a regular flight suit to me, you can find these things anywhere, especially near any air force base, do you have anything else?"

Tom reaches into the box, and pulls out the

camcorder, and replies, "Jason hook this thing up

to the television, and show Mister Anderson the

tape!"

Jason picks up the camcorder, and attaches the

video, and audio cables to it, and then he hits the

play button as the tape begins to play. The

television lights up the room, as Mason's eye open

wide, and says, "my god, that's the prospector

crew! Where did you get this tape?"

Tom replies, "it was in the crash!"

Mason who looks dumbfounded replies, "I think

we might have something here where was this tape

taken at?"

Tom replies, "well, Bill Davis was a resident in Odessa Texas, he ran a small garage, and that was taken at his house!"

Mason replies, "So the shuttle crashed near Odessa?"

Tom replies, "it must have, because it appears that Bill Davis picked them up, and they were headed towards Dallas!"

Mason who looks a bit nervous replies "I need to step out of the room and make a few calls, please excuse me!"

Mason who gets up and heads out of the room to make a few phone calls, when Jason looks over to his dad and says, "I think we got someone attention now!"

Tom who is smiling brightly, replies, "I think so son, I think so!"

After about five minutes have passed, Mason walks back into the room and says, "Tom, I'm going to take the evidence, and I need to get going!"

Mason reaches into his shirt pocket, and pulls out a business card and says, "Tom here is a card with my number on it, I will have someone to call you tomorrow, probably around 9am!"

Jason who is surprised, looks at Mason and says, "do you want to see the pictures on the camera?"

Mason replies, "Nope, I think I have seen enough, we will be in touch!"

Mason picks up the box, and heads towards the door, when Tom replies, 'Mason, where are you going in such a rush?"

Mason replies, "I'm headed to Odessa, we need to find the crash site!"

Tom looks over at Jason and says, "I think they are more worried about the crash site, than they are, about the crew!"

Jason replies, "you know what, I was thinking the same thing!"

Mason takes the box which contains the evidence, tosses it into the back of the black SUV, jumps into the driver's seat, and pulls out of the police station, and heads towards interstate twenty. He reaches the interstate and heads west towards Odessa, he hopes to find the wreckage by morning!

To be continued…..